Kissing the Witch

By the same author

Kissing the Witch

Emma Donoghue

HAMISH HAMILTON • LONDON

HAMISH HAMILTON LTD

Published by the Penguin Group
Penguin Books Ltd, 27 Wrights Lane, London w8 5tz, England
Penguin Books USA Inc., 375 Hudson Street, New York, New York 10014, USA
Penguin Books Australia Ltd, Ringwood, Victoria, Australia
Penguin Books Canada Ltd, 10 Alcorn Avenue, Toronto, Ontario, Canada m4v 3b2
Penguin Books (NZ) Ltd, 182–190 Wairau Road, Auckland 10, New Zealand

Penguin Books Ltd, Registered Offices: Harmondsworth, Middlesex, England

First published 1997
1 3 5 7 9 10 8 6 4 2
First edition

Set in 11/14.5 pt Monotype Garamond

Printed in Great Britain by Clays Ltd, St Ives plc

A CIP catalogue record for this book is available from the British Library

isbn 0–241–13676–8

To Frances,
my mother and first storyteller,
who read me Andrew Lang's 'Pinkel and the Witch'
more times than she can bear to remember,
this book is dedicated
with gratitude and love.

Acknowledgements

I want to thank Roisin Conroy of Attic Press for prompting me to write fairy tales, Siobhán Parkinson for suggesting the theme of 'The Tale of the Cottage', my agent Caroline Davidson and her apprentice Hannah Jacobmeyer for helpful criticism. *Kissing the Witch* has benefited greatly from readings and conversations with Janie Buchanan, Alison Dickens, Amy Gamble, Lara A. King, Una Ní Dhubhghaill, Gráinne Ní Dhúill, Paulina Palmer, Sandy Reeks, Chris Roulston, Sue Walker and Debra Westgate. I would also like to thank audiences in England, Ireland, Scotland and the USA for listening so responsively to these tales.

Contents

I

The Tale of the Shoe

TILL SHE CAME it was all cold.

Ever since my mother died the feather bed felt hard as a stone floor. Every word that came out of my mouth limped away like a toad. Whatever I put on my back now turned to sackcloth and chafed my skin. I heard a knocking in my skull, and kept running to the door, but there was never anyone there. The days passed like dust brushed from my fingers.

I scrubbed and swept because there was nothing else to do. I raked out the hearth with my fingernails, and scoured the floor until my knees bled. I counted grains of rice and divided brown beans from black.

Nobody made me do the things I did, nobody scolded me, nobody punished me but me. The shrill voices were all inside. Do this, do that, you lazy heap of dirt. They knew every question and answer, the voices

in my head. Some days they asked why I was still alive. I listened out for my mother but I couldn't hear her among their clamour.

When everything that could possibly be done was done for the day, the voices faded. I knelt on the hearth and looked into the scarlet cinders until my eyes swam. I was trying to picture a future, I suppose. Some nights I told myself stories to make myself weep, then stroked my own hair till I slept.

Once, out of all the times when I ran to the door and there was nobody there, there was still nobody there, but the stranger was behind me. I thought for a moment she must have come out of the fire. Her eyes had flames in their centres, and her eyebrows were silvered with ash.

The stranger said my back must be tired, and the sweeping could wait. She took me into the garden and showed me a hazel tree I had never seen before. I began to ask questions, but she put her tiny finger over my mouth so we could hear a dove murmuring on the highest branch.

It turned out that she had known my mother, when my mother was alive. She said that was my mother's tree.

How can I begin to describe the transformations?

My old dusty self was spun new. This woman sheathed my limbs in blue velvet. I was dancing on points of clear glass.

And then, because I asked, she took me to the ball. Isn't that what girls are meant to ask for?

Her carriage brought me as far as the palace steps. I knew just how I was meant to behave. I smiled ever so prettily when the great doors swung wide to announce me. I refused a canapé and kept my belly pulled in. Under the thousand crystal candelabras I danced with ten elderly gentlemen who had nothing to say but did not let that stop them. I answered only, Indeed and Oh yes and Do you think so?

At ten to twelve I came down the steps and she swept me away. Had enough? she asked, lifting a hair off my long glove.

But she was old enough to be my mother, and I was a girl with my fortune to make. The voices were beginning to jabber. They each told me to do something different. Take me back tomorrow night, I said.

So she appeared again just when the soup was boiling over, and took a silver spoon from her pocket to feed me. Our fingers drew pictures in the ashes on the hearth, vague shapes of birds and islands. She showed me the sparkle in my eyes, how wide my skirt could spread, how to waltz without getting dizzy. I was lithe in green satin now; my own mother would not have recognized me.

That night at the ball I got right into the swing of things. I tittered at the old king's jokes; I accepted a single chicken wing and nibbled it daintily. I danced three times with the prince, whose hand wavered in the small of my back. He asked me my favourite colour, but I couldn't think of any. He asked me my name, and for a moment I couldn't remember it.

At five to midnight when my feet were starting to ache I waited on the bottom step and she came for me. On the way home I leaned my head on her narrow shoulder and she put one hand over my ear. Had enough? she asked.

But I didn't have to listen to the barking voices to know how the story went: my future was about to happen. Take me back tomorrow night, I said.

So she came for me again just when the small sounds of the mice were getting on my nerves, and she told me they were coachmen to drive us in state. She claimed her little finger was a magic wand, it could do spectacular things. She could always make me laugh.

That night my new skin was red silk, shivering in the

breeze. The prince hovered at my elbow like an autumn leaf ready to fall. The musicians played the same tune over and over. I danced like a clockwork ballerina and smiled till my face twisted. I swallowed a little of everything I was offered, then leaned over the balcony and threw it all up again.

I had barely time to wipe my mouth before the prince came to propose.

Out on the steps he led me, under the half-full moon, all very fairy-tale. His long moustaches were beginning to tremble; he seemed like an actor on a creaking stage. As soon as the words began to leak out of his mouth, they formed a cloud in which I could see the future.

I could hardly hear him. The voices were shrieking yes yes yes say yes before you lose your chance you bag of nothingness.

I opened my teeth but no sound came out. There was no harm in this man: what he proposed was white and soft, comfortable as fog. There was nothing to be afraid of. But just then the midnight bell began to toll out the long procession of years, palatial day by moon-less night. And I leaped backwards down the steps, leaving one shoe behind.

The bushes tore my dress into the old rags. It was

perfectly silent on the lawn. She was waiting for me in the shadows. She didn't ask had I had enough.

I had got the story all wrong. How could I not have noticed she was beautiful? I must have dropped all my words in the bushes. I reached out.

I could hear surprise on her breath. What about the shoe? she asked.

It was digging into my heel, I told her.

What about the prince? she asked.

He'll find someone to fit, if he looks long enough.

What about me? she asked very low. I'm old enough to be your mother.

Her finger was spelling on the back of my neck.

You're not my mother, I said. I'm old enough to know that.

I threw the other shoe into the brambles, where it hung, glinting.

So then she took me home, or I took her home, or we were both somehow taken to the closest thing.

In the morning I asked,
Who were you
before you walked into my kitchen?
And she said, Will I tell you my own story?
It is a tale of a bird.

11

The Tale of the Bird

WHEN I WAS as young as you are now I learned how to save my own life. You think I have saved you, but the truth is that your need has conjured me here. It was a bird that helped me, when I was young, but it could have been anything: a stick, a stone, whatever happened by. The thing is to take your own life in your hands.

As a child I weighed mine and did not think it worth saving. Scrubbing the great steps one day, I found an old bent copper knife. In its corroded curve, my reflection was barely a thumbnail high. Now I knew for sure that I was the least thing in the world. The dogs and cats mattered more than I did. They had their places on the earth; they merited their grooming, their feeding, or their drowning; no one questioned their existence. Whereas I was not a necessary animal.

There was a man I had been taught to call father. He saw to the horses in the great stables, their bright mouths and metal chorus; his eyes never fell to my level. There was a woman who called herself my mother. She wore an apron like a snow cloud; her hands blushed red as if ashamed. I could not imagine that I had emerged from her substantial flesh; it seemed more likely that she had found me caught in a cowpat, or behind the apple barrel, or while cleaning out a mousetrap. Once, eavesdropping in the laundry, I heard her tell a neighbour that she had spent twenty years pining for a child. I could hardly have been what she had in mind.

You must understand, I was not ill-treated; no one wasted breath flinging insults at my head. I did not belong, that was all. Nor did anything belong to me; mine was a borrowed life. Considering myself as the louse in their bed, the cuckoo in their nest, I felt a certain reluctant gratitude for the food and shelter they allowed me. I wore scraps of everyone's worn-out clothing: my shoes were made of the gardener's gloves, my shift from old handkerchiefs. My names were hand-me-downs too: *girl, the creature*, or, most often, *you there*.

Every story I ever heard of changelings, babies

swapped at birth or abandoned in bulrushes, I repeated to myself at night to glean their secret message. But I had no idea how I had drifted into the path of these indifferent giants called father and mother, and I did not dare to ask.

Only in the fields did I find a sense of proportion. I knew we were all equally minute under the liquid eye of the sky, and equally precious in its sight. I used to sit so still that even the rabbits would not notice me. Seagulls wheeled overhead, gulping out their hunger. Swallows made letters against the sky, too brief to read. Once I spent a whole day there, a blade of grass in each hand to anchor me to the warm earth. I watched the sun rise, pass over my head and set. Ladybirds mated on my knuckle; a shrew nibbled a hole in my stocking while I tried not to laugh. Such a day was worth any punishment.

My mother and father beat me when they felt the need, but only by the rule of thumb: thin sticks break no bones. What they wanted, I believe, was not to hurt me, but to teach me the way things were. The lesson was simple, and if I did not learn it I had only myself to blame. The birch pen wrote it often enough on the skin of my back. Keep your horizons narrow, your expectations low, and you will never be unduly disappointed.

Keep your heart infinitesimally small, and sorrow will never spy it, never plunge, never flap away with your heart in her claws.

So when one spring in spite of all this good advice I fell in love, it felt like disaster. I took a tiny bite, and it exploded in my stomach. Love splashed through every cranny, hauled on every muscle, unlocked every joint. I was so full of astonishment, I felt ten feet tall. My shoulders itched as if wings might break through.

Little one, your skin is so soft, said the man as he stroked my cheek with one huge thumb.

I always started quivering as soon as I heard his knock at the door; when I opened it and curtsied, my knees dipped like a frog's; his first smile set me a-stutter. His eyes, cloudy under billows of black hair, were the only weak thing about him. He could always recognize me by the sound of my breathing.

Once I scrubbed the same corner for three hours, and when the man finally passed I upset my pail of dirty suds all down the passage. He stepped back at once, but his shiny leather shoes had been spattered like rocks by the seashore. I tried to wipe them with my apron, but he lifted me to my feet. Such force in his forearm; what an aimed bow was his elbow; how delicious the arc of his shoulder. His hands were backed with a faint black fur. He was like the boulder that parts the river, and he smelt like apples stored in darkness all winter.

I, who had nothing and no right to anything, would have him for my very own.

And so, somehow, it came to pass, as in the best of stories, as in the dream to which you cling like a torn blanket on an icy morning when it is past time to get up. My father, his words slurred with suspicion, told me that a great man had asked for me. My mother carried in a huge basket of linen and a needle. Unspeaking, we began to cut and sew my new life.

I would be a stain on my husband's line, I knew that without her telling. If it was his whim to stoop, to lift me up, then I was never to delude myself that I deserved it. I was always to keep in mind the tiny smoky image of what an insignificant creature I had been before he honoured me with his gaze.

But when I was presented to him, in my new dress, he made me forget all my fears. He discovered my hand in my long sleeve and began to count my fingers. No sooner had my parents backed out of the room than he was bending over me to sink his face into my hair. His whisper boomed: what were they to us, now, or we to them? His ear, against my cheek, gave off a surprising heat; my finger crawled along its furred tunnels like a venturesome bee. He would take me away from all this, he promised, give me a new name, never let anything hurt me. I began to shudder with pleasure.

The morning after our wedding, I lay awake beside the hot mountain that was my husband. I traced the brown pattern we had made on the linen: was it a flower, a claw, a snowflake? At last I decided that it was the sign of two leaves growing round each other. I belonged to him now, and he to me.

With surprising ease I learned to rule a house greater than the one I had scrubbed for my keep. I knew who I was at last: this was what I had been born for. I liked to walk through the corridors, my train of brocade sweeping the flagstones; I found delight in every pane of glass I would never have to wash. When, within the month, I found I was with child, every mirror seemed to echo my grandeur. Shameless, I longed for it to show; I wanted to be the shape of an apple or the noontime sun.

One morning at midsummer I woke early and thought I would go out to see the grass grow and the birds rise, as I used to in the days when it was my only consolation. How different I was now; how I had grown rich in things of the spirit and flesh; how my skin felt taut as a tambourine. And then my husband peered sleepily over his shoulder and asked where I was going.

It all made perfect sense the way he explained it to me as I sat on the edge of the bed: the danger of wandering under the scathing sun, the risk of exposure to rough men in the cornfields, the unsuitability of such a thing. I nodded, and laughed with him, and that morning it was true that I would rather climb into the cave of his arms and fill myself up with bliss again.

But as my hips widened the great house began to seem too small. I paced the corridors until I knew them by heart; I learned every angle of the courtyard. In their smooth leather, my feet itched for the stubble of the open fields, and my eyes strained for a far horizon.

I set out again one Sunday, when there could be no men in the fields, but still my husband said no; this time his eyes were a little bewildered. I tried again when he was away on business, but the housekeeper would not give me the key to open the gate. I sneaked off another day, while he was counting his money, and still he was gentle when they brought me back, though I could see anger stretching itself between his brows.

Again, he put it to me in words a child could understand. He enclosed my two hands in one of his huge fists, and kissed the tears from my cheeks.

I nodded. I wiped my face. I knew it was unreasonable to pine so much for a walk in the sunshine. My husband laughed softly, and wondered aloud what a breeding wife would ask for next: to fly like a kite, or a fox for a pet, or charcoal to chew on? It was only then, staring into the blur of his eyes, that it all became clear to me, and dread stopped up my mouth.

Oh, my husband was no tyrant; he would never sell my jewels, or steal my children, or cut off my head. But now I knew that what I wanted was not the same as what he wanted for me. What this good man had sworn to protect me from was not the same as what I feared. I trusted that he would never let anything hurt me, but he would never let anything touch me either.

Summer declined into chilly autumn. From my window I could see restless flocks of birds forming themselves into arrowheads, pointing south. Sometimes they faltered, broke from the shape, swung loose like hail, but always they came back together.

Day by day my belly swelled with life, but the rest of me was shrinking. My husband had taken to referring to me as if I were someone else. How is my dearest wife today? he would ask, and I would stare back mutely and think, I don't know, how is she? Where is she? Who is she? Bring her here, so I can ask her how I am to live this life.

One day he found me kneeling in a corridor, over a bundle of brown feathers. A tiny swallow: it must have flown down a chimney and battered itself to death. I was sobbing so hard he thought my time had come; he was stumbling away in search of the midwife when I turned to him and held out my hands. He peered, his face almost touching the skewed feathers, and for a moment I feared he would laugh, but his face was grave as he raised it towards me. My love, he said, what is a bird to us, or we to a bird?

I had no answer to give him. When he tried to lift me up I was too heavy for him; my legs were frozen to the ground.

As I knelt there, aware of his steps dying away, I felt a tremor under my thumbs. When I brought the bird nearer to my face, I could sense a tiny pulse. Not quite dead, then: half-way to alive.

In the week that followed, I fed the brittle creature drops of milk from my smallest fingertip and kept it warm in my fur collar. Everything waited. I refused to think about myself: my exceptional fortune, my perfect house, my excellent husband, who could make any woman happy if she let him. I simply waited to see if the bird would live.

One day it swallowed. One day it stood. One day it flew, and the next it got a glimpse of sky and tried to smash through the glass. I could have kept it beside me, a silk-tethered plaything, but what would have been the use of that?

I took it to the highest window in the house and let it out. The kick of its wings was surprisingly strong. The air smelt like frost, but there was still time to reach the summer land. I stood, watching the bird wheel over the rooftops. Flesh weighed me down like a robe. The child within me was kicking, a mute clamour for release.

Next time. Next year. I would get away somehow, sometime, with or without this child, heading somewhere I knew nothing about but that the sun would shine down on my naked head. I would be hurt and I would be fearful, but I would never be locked up again.

My life was in my own hands, now, beating faintly, too small yet for anyone to notice. I cupped freedom to my breast. I would feed it, I would love it; it would grow big enough to carry me away.

The bird circled back, and hovered outside my window for a moment as if it had something to say.

In a whisper I asked,
Who were you
before you took to the skies?
And the bird said, Will I tell you my own story?
It is a tale of a rose.

III

The Tale of the Rose

IN THIS LIFE I have nothing to do but cavort on the wind, but in my last it was my fate to be a woman.

I was beautiful, or so my father told me. My oval mirror showed me a face with nothing written on it. I had suitors aplenty but wanted none of them: their doggish devotion seemed too easily won. I had an appetite for magic, even then. I wanted something improbable and perfect as a red rose just opening.

Then in a spring storm my father's ships were lost at sea, and my suitors wanted none of me. I looked in my mirror, and saw, not myself, but every place I'd never been.

The servants were there one day and gone the next; they seemed to melt into the countryside. Last year's leaves and papers blew across the courtyard as we packed to go. My father lifted heavy trunks till veins embroidered his forehead. He found me a blanket to wrap my mirror in for the journey. My sisters held up their pale sleek fingers and complained to the wind. How could they be expected to toil with their hands?

I tucked up my skirts and got on with it. It gave me a strange pleasure to see what my back could bend to, my arms could bear. It was not that I was better than my sisters, only that I could see further.

Our new home was a cottage; my father showed me how to nail my mirror to the flaking wall. There were weeds and grasses but no roses. Down by the river, where I pounded my father's shirts white on the black rocks, I found a kind of peace. My hands grew numb and my dark hair tangled in the sunshine. I was washing my old self away; by midsummer I was almost ready.

My sisters sat just outside the door, in case a prince should ride by. The warm breeze carried the occasional scornful laugh my way.

As summer was leaving with the chilly birds, my father got word that one of his ships had come safe to shore after all. His pale eyes stood out like eggs. What he wanted most, he said, was to bring us each home whatever we wanted. My sisters asked for heavy dresses, lined cloaks, fur-topped boots, anything to keep the wind out. I knew that nothing could keep the wind out, so I asked for a red rose just opening.

The first snow had fallen before my father came home, but he did have a rose for me. My sisters waited in the doorway, arms crossed. I ran to greet him, this bent bush who was my father inching across the white ground. I took the rose into my hand before he could drop it. My father fell down. The petals were scarlet behind their skin of frost.

We piled every blanket we possessed on top of him; still his tremors shook the bed. My sisters wept and cursed, but he couldn't hear them. They cried themselves to sleep beside the fire.

That night in his delirium he raved of a blizzard and a castle, a stolen rose and a hooded beast. Then all of a sudden he was wide awake. He gripped my wrist and said, Daughter, I have sold you.

The story came wild and roundabout, in darts and flurries. I listened, fitting together the jagged pieces of my future. For a red rose and his life and a box of gold, my father had promised the beast the first thing he saw when he reached home. He had thought the first thing might be a cat. He had hoped the first thing might be a bird.

My heart pounded on the anvil of my breastbone. Father, I whispered, what does a promise mean when it is made to a monster?

He shut his trembling eyes. It's no use, he said, his tongue dry in his mouth. The beast will find us, track us down, smell us out no matter where we run. And then water ran down his cheeks as if his eyes were dissolving. Daughter, he said in a voice like old wood breaking, can you ever forgive me?

I could only answer his question with one of my own. Putting my hand over his mouth, I whispered, Which of us would not sell all we had to stay alive?

He turned his face to the wall.

Father, I said, I will be ready to leave in the morning.

Now you may tell me that I should have felt betrayed, but I was shaking with excitement. I should have felt like a possession, but for the first time in my life I seemed to own myself. I went as a hostage, but it seemed as if I was riding into battle.

I left the rose drying against my mirror, in case I ever came home. My sisters, onion-eyed, watched us leave at dawn. They couldn't understand why my father carried no gun to kill the beast. To them a word was not something to be kept. They didn't speak our language.

The castle was in the middle of a forest where the sun never shone. Every villager we stopped to ask the way spat when they heard our destination. There had been no wedding or christening in that castle for a whole generation. The young queen had been exiled, imprisoned, devoured (here the stories diverged) by a hooded beast who could be seen at sunset walking on the battlements. No one had ever seen the monster's face and lived to describe it.

We stopped to rest when the light was thinning. My father scanned the paths through the trees, trying to remember his way. His eyes swivelled like a lamb's do when the wolves are circling. He took a deep breath and began to speak, but I said, Hush.

Night fell before we reached the castle, but the light spilling from the great doors led us through the trees. The beast was waiting at the top of the steps, back to the light, swaddled in darkness. I strained to see the contours of the mask. I imagined a different deformity for every layer of black cloth.

The voice, when it came, was not cruel but hoarse, as if it had not been much used in twenty years. The beast asked me, Do you come consenting?

I did. I was sick to my stomach, but I did.

My father's mouth opened and shut a few times, as

if he was releasing words that the cold air swallowed up. I kissed his papery cheek and watched him ride away. His face was lost in the horse's mane.

Though I explored the castle from top to bottom over the first few days, I found no trace of the missing queen. Instead there was a door with my name on it, and the walls of my room were white satin. There were a hundred dresses cut to my shape. The great mirror showed me whatever I wanted to see. I had keys to every room in the castle except the one where the beast slept. The first book I opened said in gold letters: You are the mistress: ask for whatever you wish.

I didn't know what to ask for. I had a room of my own, and time and treasures at my command. I had everything I could want except the key to the story.

Only at dinner was I not alone. The beast liked to watch me eat. I had never noticed myself eating before; each time I swallowed, I blushed.

At dinner on the seventh night, the beast spoke. I knocked over my glass, and red wine ran the length of the table. I don't remember what the words were. The voice came out muffled and scratchy from behind the mask.

After a fortnight, we were talking like the wind and the roof slates, the rushes and the river, the cat and the mouse. The beast was always courteous; I wondered what scorn this courtesy veiled. The beast was always gentle; I wondered what violence hid behind this gentleness.

I was cold. The wind wormed through the shutters. I was lonely. In all this estate there was no one like me. But I had never felt so beautiful.

I sat in my satin-walled room, before the gold mirror. I looked deep into the pool of my face, and tried to imagine what the beast looked like. The more hideous my imaginings, the more my own face seemed to glow. Because I thought the beast must be everything I was not: dark to my light, rough to my smooth, hoarse to my sweet. When I walked on the battlements under the waning moon, the beast was the grotesque shadow I threw behind me.

One night at dinner the beast said, You have never seen my face. Do you still picture me as a monster?

I did. The beast knew it.

By day I sat by the fire in my white satin room reading tales of wonder. There were so many books on so many shelves, I knew I could live to be old without coming to the end of them. The sound of the pages turning was the sound of magic. The dry liquid feel of paper under fingertips was what magic felt like.

One night at dinner the beast said, You have never felt my touch. Do you still shrink from it?

I did. The beast knew it.

At sunset I liked to wrap up in furs and walk in the rose garden. The days were stretching, the light was lingering a few minutes longer each evening. The rose-bushes held up their spiked fingers against the yellow sky, caging me in.

One night at dinner the beast asked, What if I let you go? Would you stay of your own free will?

I would not. The beast knew it.

And when I looked in the great gold mirror that night, I thought I could make out the shape of my father, lying with his feverish face turned to the ceiling. The book did say I was to ask for whatever I wanted.

I set off in the morning. I promised to return on the eighth day, and I meant it when I said it.

Taking leave on the steps, the beast said, I must tell you before you go: I am not a man.

I knew it. Every tale I had ever heard of trolls, ogres, goblins, rose to my lips.

The beast said, You do not understand.

But I was riding away.

The journey was long, but my blood was jangling bells. It was dark when I reached home. My sisters were whispering over the broth. My father turned his face to me and tears carved their way across it. The rose, stiff against the mirror, was still red.

By the third day he could sit up in my arms. By the fifth day he was eating at table and patting my knee. On the seventh day my sisters told me in whispers that it would surely kill him if I went back to the castle. Now I had paid my ransom, they said, what could possess me to return to a monster? My father's eyes followed me round the cottage.

The days trickled by and it was spring. I pounded shirts on black rocks down by the river. I felt young again, as if nothing had happened, as if there had never been a door with my name on it.

But one night I woke to find myself sitting in front of my mirror. In its dark pool I thought I could see the castle garden, a late frost on the trees, a black shape on the grass. I found the old papery rose clenched in my fist, flaking into nothing.

This time I asked no permission of anyone. I kissed my dozing father and whispered in his ear. I couldn't tell if he heard me. I saddled my horse, and was gone before first light.

It was sunset when I reached the castle, and the doors were swinging wide. I ran through the grounds, searching behind every tree. At last I came to the rose garden, where the first buds were hunched against the night air. There I found the beast, a crumpled bundle eaten by frost.

I pulled and pulled until the padded mask lay uppermost. I breathed my heat on it, and kissed the spot I had warmed. I pulled off the veils one by one. Surely it couldn't matter what I saw now?

I saw hair black as rocks under water. I saw a face white as old linen. I saw lips red as a rose just opening.

I saw that the beast was a woman. And that she was breathing, which seemed to matter more.

This was a strange story, one I would have to learn a new language to read, a language I could not learn except by trying to read the story.

I was a slow learner but a stubborn one. It took me days to learn that there was nothing monstrous about this woman who had lived alone in a castle, setting all her suitors riddles they could make no sense of, refusing to do the things queens are supposed to do, until the day when, knowing no one who could see her true face, she made a mask and from then on showed her face to no one. It took me weeks to understand why the faceless mask and the name of a beast might be chosen over all the great world had to offer. After months of looking, I saw that beauty was infinitely various, and found it behind her white face.

I struggled to guess these riddles and make sense of our story, and before I knew it summer was come again, and the red roses just opening.

And as the years flowed by, some villagers told travellers of a beast and a beauty who lived in the castle and could be seen walking on the battlements, and others told of two beauties, and others, of two beasts.

Another summer in the rose garden, I asked,
Who were you
before you chose a mask over a crown?
And she said, Will I tell you my own story?
It is a tale of an apple.

IV

The Tale of the Apple

THE MAID WHO brought me up told me that my mother was restless. She said I had my mother's eyes, always edging towards the steep horizon, and my mother's long hands, never still. As the story went, my mother sat one day beside an open window looking out over the snow, embroidering coronets on a dress for the christening of the child she carried. The maid warned her that she'd catch her death if she sat in the cold, letting snow drift in and sprinkle her work. My mother didn't seem to hear. Just then the needle drove itself into her finger, and three drops of blood stained the snow on the ebony window frame. My mother said to her maid, The daughter I carry will have hair as black as ebony, lips as red as blood, skin as white as snow. What will she have that will save her from my fate?

The maid had no answer, or not one that she could remember.

Then the pains seized my mother and carried her away.

Though I was so much smaller than she was, I was stronger; I had no reason not to want to live.

It was the maid who cared for me as I grew. Every autumn in her pocket she brought me the first apple from the orchard. This was not the mellow globe they served my father a month later, but the hardly bearable tang of the first ripening, so sharp it made me shudder.

Let it be said that my father did grow to care. After the maid, too, died in her turn, he found me wandering the draughty corridors of the castle and took me up in his ermine arms. In the summertime he liked to carry me through the orchard and toss me high in the air, then swing me low over the green turf. He was my toyman and my tall tree. As I grew and grew, he bounced me on his lap till our cheeks scalded.

But the day there was a patch of red on my crumpled sheet, my father brought home a new wife. She was not many years older than I was, but she had seen one royal husband into the grave already. She had my colouring. Her face was set like a jewel in a ring. I could see she was afraid; she kissed me and spoke sweetly in front of the whole court, but I could tell she would be my enemy. There was room for only one queen in a castle.

Yes, I handed this newcomer the ring with its hundred tinkling keys, the encrusted coronet, the velvet train of state, till she was laden down with all the apparatus of power. But it was me the folk waved to as the carriage rattled by; it was me who was mirrored in my father's fond eyes; mine was the first apple from the orchard.

I know now that I would have liked her if we could have met as girls, ankle deep in a river. I would have taken her hand in mine if I had not found it weighted down by the ruby stolen from my mother's cooling finger. I could have loved her if, if, if.

Her lips were soft against my forehead when she kissed me in front of the whole court. But I knew from the songs that a stepmother's smile is like a snake's, so I shut my mind to her from that very first day when I was rigid with the letting of first blood.

In the following months she did all she could to woo my friendship, and I began to soften. I thought perhaps I had misread the tight look in her eyes. Eventually I let her dress me up in the silks and brocades she had brought over the mountains. It was she who laced up my stays every morning till I was pink with mirth;

last thing at night it was she who undid the searing laces one by one and loosed my flesh into sleep. With her own hands she used to work the jewelled comb through my hair, teasing out the knots. Not content with all this, she used to feed me fruit from her own bowl, each slice poised between finger and thumb till I was ready to take it. Though I never trusted her, I took delight in what she gave me.

My father was cheered to see us so close. Once when he came to her room at night he found us both there, cross-legged on her bed under a sea of velvets and laces, trying how each earring looked against the other's ear. He put his head back and laughed to see us. Two such fair ladies, he remarked, have never been seen on one bed. But which of you is the fairest of them all?

We looked at each other, she and I, and chimed in the chorus of his laughter. Am I imagining in retrospect that our voices rang a little out of tune? You see, her hair was black as coal, mine as ebony. My lips were red as hers were, and our cheeks as pale as two pages of a book closed together. But our faces were not the same, and not comparable.

He let out another guffaw. Tell me, he asked, how am I to judge between two such beauties?

I looked at my stepmother, and she stared back at me, and our eyes were like mirrors set opposite each other, making a corridor of reflections, infinitely hollow.

My father grinned as he kissed me on the forehead, and pushed me gently out of the room, and bolted the door behind me.

But as the full of a year went by and my stepmother stayed as thin as the day he had first brought her to the castle, my father's mouth began to stiffen. He questioned every doctor who passed through the mountains. He made his young wife drink cow's blood, to strengthen her, though it turned her stomach. Finally he forbade her to go walking in the orchard with me, or lift a hand, or do anything except lie on her back and wait to find herself with child, the child who would be his longed-for son.

My stepmother lay on her back and grew so limp I could see the bones below her eyes. When I brought her red-bound books and jewelled earrings she turned her face away. I took to walking in the orchard on my own again, and once or twice boredom drove me a little way into the forest that lay beyond the castle walls. Fear enlivened those afternoons; I kept my back to the light and turned my head at every creak of wind. The forest was like a foreign court, with its own unspoken rules. The birches moved to a music only they could hear; the oaks wanted for nothing, needed no touch.

As another year stretched into spring it was not my stepmother who lay swollen and sick, but my father. He curled up on his side like a bear troubled by flies. I stood by his bed, on and off, but he was past caring. He cursed the doctors, he cursed his enemies, he cursed the two wives who had failed him, and finally with a wet mouth he cursed the son who had never come.

My stepmother had me called to the throne room where she sat, huddled in ermine, fist closed around the sceptre.

Say that I am queen, she said.

You are my father's wife, I replied.

I will be queen after he is dead, she said.

I made no reply.

Say that I am queen, she repeated, her fingers whitening around the sceptre.

If you really were, I told her, it would need no saying.

She stood on the pedestal above me. The moment I am a widow, she said, I could have you cast out.

Indeed.

If you cross me in this, she said confidingly, I could

have a huntsman take you into the forest, chop out your heart, and bring it back on a plate.

Strong meat, I murmured.

I can do it, she howled. I have the power.

I said nothing.

She lashed out with the sceptre, but I stepped back, and it crashed to the floor. I was gone before it rolled to a halt.

That night I heard many feet hammer a track to my father's room. I flattened my face into my pillow. I waited. No sound cutting through the dark castle; no final word for me. The linen lay against my eyelids, still dry.

I decided not to stay to see what the day of the funeral would bring, which courtiers' eyes would shine with flattery, and which glitter with violence. I decided to leave it all to her, and leave her to it. I filled my hems with gold pieces and slipped away.

If it had been winter still, that first night would have finished me; only the mild air was my salvation. Wider than I ever imagined, the forest was home to creatures I couldn't put names to, things with silver eyes and audible teeth; for all my furs, I didn't sleep a wink that night. By sunrise I was more lost than any nestling. All my plans came to nothing: I never found the family of the maid who had raised me, nor an empty cottage to live in. Everything I put my tongue to tasted like poison.

After wandering half starved and half crazed for more days than I can remember, I had the good fortune to be taken in by a gang of woodsmen.

They put water to my stained lips and asked who I was. The truth was quicker than a lie, so I told it. They nodded. They had heard of the death of the king. One of them asked what was in my skirts to make them so heavy, and I said, Knives, and he took his hand off my thigh and never touched me again.

That first night they fed me, and every other night I fed them. Though squat and surly, with earth in every line of their faces, these were not bad men, and considering how little my condition entitled me to, they treated me royally.

I guessed how to cook the food they threw on the table, gathering together from the shattered jigsaw of memory everything I must have seen the castle servants do ten thousand times. Gradually I learned how to keep hunger at bay and disease from the door: all the sorcery of fire and iron and water.

Hard work was no hardship to me; it kept the pictures at bay. Whenever I slackened or stopped to rest by the fire, I was haunted by the image of my step-mother. My father was only a tiny picture in my mind, shut away like a miniature in a locket. But his young widow stalked behind my eyes, growing tall or wide as I let my mind dwell on her, now smiling, now spitting, ever stretching like a shadow against a wall. I pictured her life as the queen of the castle, and it was strangely familiar: long days in charge of fire, and iron, and water. Her hands would stay smooth as lilies while mine were scrubbed raw day by day, but we were living much the same kind of life.

The men never asked what was in my mind, not even when I got lost in a daze and let the broth burn. They let me dream by the fire like a cat.

This was only a lull, a time out of time. You see, I knew my stepmother would find me. The thread between us was stretched thin, wound round trees and snagged in thickets, but never broken. Somehow I trusted she would track me down and kill me.

But when she came at last she seemed to have changed. I looked out over the half door one summer day and there she stood in the clearing, hitching her horse to a tree. There was nothing of the wife about her when she smiled. May I come into your house? she asked.

I said no and turned away. But when I had stoked up the fire and boiled the shirts and chopped the turnips, I went back to the door, out of curiosity, and she was still there, with her back to the tree.

I let her in for a minute. She said how thin I had grown. I said I was well. We said not a word of what was past. She said, I keep breaking mirrors.

Sitting by the fire with her I shut my eyes and it felt like old times. She stood behind me and laced up my stays tightly, the way I could never lace them on my own.

When they came home that night the men found me alone in a sort of stupor. First they were anxious, to hear my breath come so quick and shallow, and then they were angry, to see the turnips curling on the table and no food in the pot. They said my stepmother had to be a sorceress, to find me so deep in the forest.

Some weeks went by and I was myself again, scrubbing and mashing and earning my keep. The visit began to seem like another one of my daydreams.

One afternoon I was resting on a tree stump outside the cottage, snatching a moment of sun on my back, when I heard the jangle of her harness. This time, she knelt beside me, and there was nothing of the queen about her. I haven't had a night's sleep since you left, she said; it feels like dancing in shoes of red-hot iron. Will you come home now?

I said, No, and turned my head away. She took out her jewelled comb and began to draw it through my hair, patient with all the burs and knots my new life had put in it. I shut my eyes and let the points of the comb dig into my scalp, scraping down to the kernel of memory.

When they came home that night the men found me curled around the tree stump on the damp grass. They lifted me up and told me that my stepmother must be a witch to put such poison of idleness in my head. They warned me to stay inside and shut the door to all comers.

For some weeks I did what I was told, kept house and kept quiet. My hair knotted again, my stays hung loose.

But one afternoon in early autumn I was troubled by a whiff of a scent of overpowering sharpness. I could not remember what it was; all I knew was that I could hardly stand it. I turned, and there at the half door my stepmother stood, an apple in her upturned hand.

Stepmother, yes, that was the word, but there was nothing of the mother about her.

The apple was half ripe. One side was green, the

other red. She bit into the green side and swallowed and smiled. I took the apple from her without a word, bit into the red side, and began to choke. Fear and excitement locked in struggle in my throat, and blackness seeped across my eyes. I fell to the ground.

It was all white, where I went; like warm snow, packed into the angles and crevices of my body. There was no light, or noise, or colour. I thought I was treasure, stowed away for safe keeping.

When I came to I was jolting along in an open coffin. Sunlight stabbed my eyelids. The woodsmen were bearing me down the mountain, out of the woods. I gagged, coughed, sat up. How their eyes rounded; how they laughed to see me breathing. But lie down, one said, you are not well yet. Until you were poisoned we had been forgetting who you are, said a second; now we're taking you to another kingdom, where they'll know how to treat a princess. Lie down and rest, little one, said a third; we have a long way to go.

My head was still swimming; I thought I might faint again. But my mouth was full of apple, slippery, still hard, vinegary at the edges. I could feel the marks of my own teeth on the skin. I bit down, and juice ran to the corners of my lips. It was not poisoned. It was the first apple of the year from my father's orchard. I chewed till it was eaten up and I knew what to do.

I made them set me down, and I got out of the box, deaf to their clamour. I stared around me till I could see the castle, tiny against the flame-coloured forest, away up the hill. I turned my face towards it, and started walking.

In the orchard, I asked,
Who were you
before you married my father?
And she said, Will I tell you my own story?
It is a tale of a handkerchief.

V

The Tale of the Handkerchief

THE REASON I would have killed you to stay a queen is that I have no right to be a queen. I have been a fraud from the beginning.

I was born a maid, daughter to a maid, in the court of a widow far across the mountains. How could you, a pampered princess, know what it's like to be a servant, a pair of hands, a household object? To be no one, to own nothing, to owe every last mouthful to those you serve?

All our queen loved in the world was her horse and her daughter.

The horse was white, a magnificent mare with a neck like an oak. The princess was born in the same month of the same year as I was. But where I was dark, with thick brows that overshadowed my bright eyes, the princess was fair. Yellowish, I thought her; slightly transparent, as if the sun had never seen her face. All she liked to do was walk in the garden, up and down the shady paths between the hedges. Once when I was picking nettles for soup, I saw her stumble on the gravel and bruise her knee. The queen ran into the garden at the first cry, lifted her on to her lap and wiped two jewelled tears away with her white handkerchief. Another time I was scrubbing a hearth and stood up to stretch my back, when laughter floated through the open window. I caught sight of the two of them cantering past on the queen's horse, their hands dancing in its snowy mane.

My own mother died young and tired, having made me promise to be a good maid for the rest of my days. I kissed her waxy forehead and knew that I would break my word.

But for the moment I worked hard, kept my head low and my apron clean. At last I was raised to the position of maid to the princess. Telling me of my good fortune, the queen rested her smooth hand for half a moment on my shoulder. If your mother only knew, she said, how it would gladden her heart.

The young princess was a gentle mistress, never having needed to be anything else. The year she came of age, the queen received ambassadors from all the neighbouring kingdoms. The prince she chose for her daughter lived a long day's ride away. He was said to be young enough. The girl said neither yes nor no; it was not her question to answer. She stood very still as I tried the bridal dresses on her for size. My hands looked like hen's claws against the shining brocade. The queen told her daughter not to be sad, never to be wilful, and always to remember her royal blood. I listened, my mouth full of pins.

If I had had such a mother I would never have left her to journey into a strange country. I would have fought and screamed and clung to the folds of her cloak. But then, my blood is not royal.

Ahead of her daughter the queen sent gold and silver and a box full of crystals. She took the princess into the chamber where I was packing furs, and there she took out a knife and pressed the point into her own finger. I could hardly believe it; I almost cried out to stop her. The queen let three drops of blood fall on to her lawn handkerchief. She tucked this into the girl's bosom, saying that as long as she kept the handkerchief, she could come to no great harm.

And then the queen led her daughter out into the courtyard, and swung her up on to her own great horse. I would come with you myself, she said, if only my kingdom were secure. In these troubled times, you will be safer where you're going. In my place, you will have my own horse to carry you, and your own maid to ride behind you.

This was the first I had heard of it. I went to pack my clean linen. The rest of my bits and pieces I left under the mattress for the next maid; I had nothing worth taking into a far country. In the courtyard, a stableman hoisted me on to a nag weighed down with all the princess's paraphernalia.

I watched the queen and the princess kiss goodbye in the early-morning sunlight. The horse's mane shone like a torch, but where the mother's forehead rested against the daughter's, the sun behind them was blotted out.

We trotted along for some hours without speaking; the princess seemed lost in daydreams, and my mother had taught me never to be the first to break a silence. The day grew hotter as the sun crawled up the sky. Sweat began to break through the princess's white throat, trickling down the neck of her heavy gold dress. My thin smock was scorching through.

Suddenly there was a glint in the trees. The princess brought her great white horse to a halt and said, without looking at me, Please fill my golden cup with some cool water from that stream.

The heat in my head was a hammer on an anvil, pounding a sword into shape. It was the first order I ever disobeyed in my life. If you're thirsty, I told her, get it yourself.

The princess turned her milky face and stared at me. When my eyes refused to fall she climbed down, a little awkwardly, and untied her cup. She pulled back her veil as she walked to the stream. I was thirsty myself, but I didn't move. The white horse looked round at me with its long eyes that seemed to say, If her mother only knew, it would break her heart. When the princess walked back from the stream, her mouth was wet and her cheeks were pale.

We rode on for several hours until the sun was beginning to sink. The princess reined in at the edge of a river and asked me again, more shyly, if I would fetch her some water. I did mean to say yes this time, now that I had taught her a lesson; I was not plotting anything. But when I opened my mouth the sound that came out was No. If you want to drink, I said hoarsely, you have to stoop down for it.

I held her gaze until her eyes fell. She got down and stepped through the rushes to the water. The horse tossed its foam-coloured head and neighed as if warning of an enemy approach. My lips were cracked; my tongue rasped against them as I watched the princess. She bent over the stream to fill her cup, and something fluttered from the curve of her breast into the water. My handkerchief, she cried, as it slid away. As if saying what it was would bring it back.

With that I leaped down from my knock-kneed horse and waded into the river. I found the square of linen caught in a knot of reeds, mud silting over the three brown drops. I turned and shook it in the princess's face. A drop of water caught on her golden sleeve. You know nothing, I told her. Do you even know how to wash a handkerchief?

She shook her head. Her cheeks were marked with red, like faint roads on a map.

You scrub it on a rock like this, I told her, and scrub again, and scrub harder, and keep scrubbing until your fingers are numb. Look, the spots are coming out. Your mother's royal blood is nearly gone.

The princess made a small moan.

Look, there are only three faint marks left, I said. And then you find somewhere off the ground and leave it to bleach in the sun, I instructed her, tossing the handkerchief up into the high branches of a tree.

The princess's eyes left the handkerchief and came

back. Hers was the look of the rabbit and it brought out all the snake in me. Take off your dress, I told her.

She blinked.

Take off your dress or I'll strip it from your body with my bare hands.

She reached behind to unfasten the hooks. I didn't help. I watched. Then I slipped my own plain dress over my head. The air felt silken on my shoulders. The dresses lay crumpled at our feet like snakeskins. Look, I said. Where is the difference between us now?

The princess had no answer.

I picked up the golden cup and filled it from the stream. I drank until my throat hurt. I splashed my face and arms and breasts until I shivered despite the sun. Then I stepped into the stiff golden dress and turned my back on the girl. After a moment she understood, and began to do up the hooks and eyes. When she was finished, she hesitated, then pulled on the smock I had left in a heap by the rushes. It suited her. Her fair hair hung around her dry lips. I filled the cup again and passed it to her. She drank without a word.

When I got on to the white horse, it reared under me, and I had to give it a kick to make it stand still. I waited until I could hear the girl settling in the saddle of the old nag, and then I wheeled around. I am the queen's daughter, I told her, and you are my maid, and if you ever say otherwise I will rip your throat open with my bare hands.

Her eyes slid down to my fingers. The skin was angry, with calluses on the thumbs; anyone who saw it would know. I rummaged around in the saddlebag until I found a pair of white gloves and pulled them on. The girl was looking away. I moved my great horse alongside hers, until I was so close I could have struck her. Swear by the open sky, I whispered, that you will never tell anyone what has happened by this river.

I swear by the open sky, she repeated doubtfully, raising her eyes to it.

We rode on. The gold dress was heavier than I could have imagined. My bones felt as if they had been made to bear this burden, as if they had found their one true dress at last.

It was dark by the time we reached the palace. They had lit a double row of torches for us to follow. The prince came to the foot of the steps and lifted me down from my horse. Through the hard brocade I couldn't feel whether he was warm or cold. He was pale with nerves but he had a kind face. At the top of the steps I made him put me down. I said, The maid I brought with me.

Yes? His voice was thin but not unpleasant.

She does not know anything about waiting on ladies. Could you set her to some simpler task?

Perhaps she could mind the geese, suggested the prince.

I gave a single nod and walked beside him towards the great doors. My back prickled. If the girl was going to denounce me this would be the moment for it. But I heard nothing except the clinking harnesses as they led the horses away.

I found that I knew how to behave like a princess, from my short lifetime of watching. I snapped my fan; I offered my gloved hand to be kissed; I never bent my back. At times, I forgot for a moment that I was acting.

But I never forgot to be afraid. I had wanted to be married at once, but the pace of royal life is stately. There were pigs to be fattened, spices to wait for, the king and his army to come safely home. I was given a broad chamber with a view of the city arch and all the fields beyond.

The first week slid by. The goose girl seemed to go about her duties without a word. I had never eaten such good food in my life, but my stomach was a knotted rope. Every day I made some excuse to pass by the stables and catch a glimpse of the great white horse in its box. Its eyes grew longer as they fixed on me. If the queen her mother only knew, they seemed to say.

I became convinced that it was the horse who would betray me. It was not scared the way the goose girl was. In the dreams that came to ride me in my gilt feather bed, the horse drew pictures in the mud under the city arch with its hoof, illustrating my crime for all the court to see. Sometimes it spoke aloud in my head, its voice a deep whistle, telling all it knew. I woke with my knees under my chin, as if I were packed in a barrel, as we punish thieves in these mountains. That evening at dinner I said to my pale fiancé, That brute of a horse I rode here tried to throw me on the journey.

Then we will have it destroyed, he assured me.

His eyes were devoted, the shape of almonds. He looked as if he would believe every word that slipped from my mouth.

The next day, I passed by the stableyard, and the box was empty. Back in my chamber, I threw the window open to the delicate air. My eye caught sight of something bright, nailed to the city arch. Something the shape of a horse's head. Below it stood a girl, geese clacking at her skirts. From this distance I couldn't be sure if her lips were moving.

She must have bribed the knacker to save the horse's head and nail it up where she would pass by. She must have guessed the exact shape of my fears. I watched her make her way through the arch and out into the open fields.

Another week crawled by. Every day I looked out for the girl pausing under the arch with her noisy flock, and tried to read her face. I wore my finest dresses, but my heart was drumming under their weight. I kept my white gloves buttoned, even on the hottest days.

I began to worry that the queen might come to the wedding after all, as a surprise for her daughter, despite the danger of leaving her kingdom unguarded. In the dreams that lined up along my bed, the queen pointed at me across the royal dining table and slapped the crown from my head. She ripped the glove from my hand and held up my finger, pressing it to the point of her knife, till dark drops stained the tablecloth: See, she cried, there is nothing royal about this blood, common as dirt. When I woke, doubled up, I felt as if they were driving long spikes through the sides of the barrel, into my skin.

One day I heard that a messenger had come from the kingdom of my birth. I couldn't get to him before the prince did. I sat in my chamber, waiting for the heavy tramp of the guards. But the step, when it came at last, was soft. The prince said, The queen your mother has fallen in battle.

So she will not be coming to the wedding? I asked, and only then understood his words. I bent over to hide my face from him; his gentle eyes shamed me. I hoped my laughter would sound like tears. And then the tears did come, and I hoped they were for her, a queen dead in her prime, and not just for my own treacherous self.

I don't know who told the goose girl. I had not the courage. I suppose she heard it in the kitchen, or from a goose boy. I thought that the moment of hearing might be the moment she would run through the court to denounce me. But the next morning she was standing under the arch in the usual way, her face turned up as if in conversation with the rotting head above her. She paused no longer than usual before walking her flock into the fields.

The day before the wedding I rode out into the country. I found myself near the river where it all began, this fantastical charade. I stopped beside the bank, and there in the tree above my head was a flash of white.

I had to take off my dress to climb, or I would have got stuck in the branches. The tree left red lashes on my arms and thighs. At last my hand reached the handkerchief. It was washed through by the dew and bleached stiff by the sun, but there were still three faint brown marks.

I saw then that the end was coming. When I had dressed myself I rode straight for the fields around the castle to find the goose girl. All at once I knew it would be tonight she would tell them; she was waiting till the last minute, so my hopes would be at their highest just before the guards came to take me away to a walled-up, windowless room.

There she was with the breeze blowing her yellow hair out of its bonds and across her sunburned face. I rode up to her, then jumped down. I held out the handkerchief; my hand was shaking. It still bears the marks of your mother's royal blood, I told her. If I give it to you now, will you let me run away before you tell them?

She tucked the handkerchief into her rough dress and said, Tell what?

I stared at her. Your fear of me will die away, I said. Your need to speak the truth will swell within you. You will be overheard lamenting as you sleep beside the stove; you will confide in the reeds and they will sing it back.

Her eyes flicked upwards. She said, By the open sky, I swear I will never tell what is not true.

But you are the royal princess, I reminded her.

A little time passed before she spoke. No, she said, I don't think so, not any more. The horse helped me to understand.

What?

When it was alive, it seemed to be a proud and stern horse, she said. After you had it killed, I could hear it talking in my head, and what it had to say surprised me.

My mouth was hanging open.

I've grown accustomed to this life, the goose girl went on. I have found the fields are wider than any garden. I was always nervous, when I was a princess, in case I would forget what to do. You fit the dresses better; you carry it off.

My mouth was dry; I shut it. I could hardly believe her words, this unlooked-for reprieve. If your mother only knew, I protested, it would break her heart.

My mother is dead, said the girl, and she knows everything now.

When I heard her, the barrel I felt always around my

ribs seemed to crack open, its hoops ringing about my feet. I could breathe. I could stretch.

That night at dinner the prince filled my goblet with the best wine, and I gave him a regal smile. He had very clean fingernails and the blue pallor of true royalty. He was all I needed. Perhaps I would even grow to love him in the end, once I was truly safe; stranger things had happened. Once I had the crown settled on my head and a baby or two on my lap, who knew what kind of woman I might turn out to be? That night I slept deep and dreamless.

During the wedding, my mind wandered. I looked out of the chapel window, on to the rooftops. From here I couldn't see the city arch, or the wide yellow fields. I wondered how the goose girl had felt when she heard the wedding bells. I thought of how both of us had refused to follow the paths mapped out for us by our mothers and their mothers before them, but had perversely gone our own ways instead, and I wondered whether this would bring us more or less happiness in the end.

Then I heard a tiny cough. When the prince took his lace handkerchief away from his mouth, there was a spatter of blood on it. I gave my husband a proper, searching look for the first time. I saw the red rims of his eyes, the hollows of his cheeks. Once more I seemed to feel the barrel locked around me, the spikes hammering through. I knew if I was not with child in a month or two, I would have nothing to hold on to. The day after my husband's funeral I would be wandering the world again in search of a crown I could call my own.

Passing one day under the arch I looked
up and asked the grin of bone,
Who were you
before the queen chose you as her horse?
And the horse said, Will I tell you my own story?
It is a tale of hair.

VI

The Tale of the Hair

Y OU SEE ME now reduced to a skull; I have shed all the trappings of flesh, skin and mane. You'll look much like this when you're dead too. How slight our differences become, between lives. In my last life I was not a horse, but a woman like you. Or rather, a woman quite unlike you. Where you hunger for attention, I sickened of it. You want to be queen over the wide world; I hid away from it.

When I was a girl I used to live in a tower. It was a misshapen tree of stone, hidden in a forest; it was mine. The woman who built it was not my mother. Sometimes she would say that she had found me growing in a clump of wild garlic; other times, that she had won me in a bet; other times, that she had bought me for a handful of radishes. Once she claimed that she had saved me, without saying from what.

I remember nothing of my early childhood except the odd glimpse of rust on a gate, butter in a churn. I knew what a town was, and a plough, and a baby, though I couldn't remember ever having laid eyes on these things. The woman said there must have been a time when my eyes were not clouded, but from the day I fell into her hands I was blind as a mole. Before there was ever a tower, we lived in a stone hut in the woods, near an old mine.

The only thing I had from the time before, the only thing I owned that the woman had not given me, was a comb made out of an antler. I liked to sit beside the window of our cottage so the air brightened a little in front of my face. With the comb I used to form my long hair into a sheet, then into coils as slick as the stream that wound through the woods.

The woman was my store of knowledge, my cache of wisdom. Which was odd, since she had so little to say, and what she spoke was never above a whisper, for fear of disturbing the birds and the beasts. She taught me you only have the right to kill a creature when you know its names and ways. She walked out in all weathers, and never shrank from the cold. Sometimes she spoke of her childhood in a country so frozen that people could walk on water. When she murmured of such things under her breath, it was as if I could see them.

As the years pulled me towards womanhood my body swelled, my spirits whirled. My hair began to grow faster; one day I could sit on its sharp ends, and another day again, I could cover my knees with it. I felt its weight pulling at the back of my head; it lolled like curtains over my cheeks.

I was never warm enough; too little of the day ever reached down through the trees to our cottage. Once when the woman came back with a bowl of milk from a sheep that had strayed into the woods, I said, I wish I could live up there in the light, in a high tower.

What do you want light for if not to see by? she asked.

All I could answer was: I like the feel of it on my face.

As ever, the woman did what I asked, without asking anything in return, but it was the first time she had not understood me.

With her weathered hands she brought stones from the old mine and took mud and leaves and built a little tower behind our hut where the thorn-bushes grew. When I shook my head out of the first window she had made, my hair spilled down. The woman laughed as she walked by; I felt the pull of her hand like a fish through the rapids of my hair. Higher, I crowed.

So she fetched more stones from the old mine and built another room on top of that, and then another, till the round wall hoisted itself up almost as high as the trees. At last the woman climbed down the steps; I heard her wipe the crust of mud from her hands on a tree. She complained that the tower was all askew, but when I stood at the base and stretched my arms around its jagged girth, I knew it was just what I needed.

We went back to our old life, except that as I shelled nuts and chopped roots in the highest room of the tower the light was white against my face. The woman came and went, bringing limp rabbits from her traps and the odd handful of berries. We didn't talk much, she and I. Often a whole day would go by with no need for naming things.

But the time I first bled I had a nightmare of the hunt. The wood was full of men who were also stags and also the dogs that chased them. My hair was caught in a tangle of hedge, my clothes shredded by the thorns. There was no safety. There was no cover. There was no door to the tower, when in my dream I stumbled through the thorn-bushes and found it at last, clubbing my fists on the stone walls to be let in. I woke only when the woman came upstairs, pulled my hands from the stones, and took me in her arms as she had never done before. She held me till I slept, whispering in my ear all the names of the herbs.

The next day the trees were no friends of mine. They slouched on the edge of our clearing, wrapping their arms round themselves and hissing in the wind. I stood in the door of the hut and shook, in spite of my coat of rabbit skins. Even my hair, wound round and round my shoulders, couldn't keep me warm.

By the time the woman came back from her plot of beans and potatoes, I had climbed up the narrow stone steps and sat by the window. Even if I'd had my sight, the woman always said there was nothing but treetops to see. I shook my hair off my shoulders now; it slid over the dusty sill.

The woman climbed up and stood behind me. I could tell her heavy step on the stone, the smell of sheep's wool on her back, wild garlic on her fingertips. I told her, I'm afraid of the forest.

But the forest is what we eat, she said. What we wear. What we burn.

I told her, I can't rest for fear of the wind and the wolves and the hunting horn.

Do you think I'd let you be hurt? she asked. Trust my ears to hear the horn, and my fire to scare the wolves, and my arms to keep out the wind.

But I trusted nothing but stone. Block up the window below me, I begged her, and the window below that, and all the windows there are except this one.

Though she must have thought me mad, she did it. Every night now I slept safe by the highest window among the tossing leaves. The woman preferred her heap of furs at the bottom of the tower; she had no taste for heights.

The door at the foot of the tower could still open, but why would I climb down, when the woman brought me anything I needed? Sometimes to save her legs I leaned out of the window and let down a basket on a rope I had woven of old rags; she said my stray hairs, knotted into it, glinted like gold thread.

I sat in the high room and chopped radishes, singing to amuse myself. I sang of the moon and a prince and a ring. The woman called up from where she was skinning a fox. Where did you hear of such things?

In the stories.

What stories? she said. I never told you such stories. Who's been telling you stories?

I must have heard them in the time before.

She said, You have never even seen a man.

No, I answered, but I can imagine.

I could hear the weight of her feet stomping into the woods, and I sang on.

> *Sprinkle him with lavender*
> *Gird his throat with gold*
> *For her royal lover rides to see her*
> *On his charger so bold*

Crude rhymes, but they pleased me, as I let the chopping knife drop and set to loosening and combing and replaiting my hair.

And then like an answer to my songs he came. It was late one night, the time when I felt least the gap between sight and lack of sight. At the end of the verse a voice came up from the forest floor. Who is it who sings so beautifully? it asked. Come to the window that I may see your face.

I sat like stone. By the time I dragged my feet to the window and called down, there was no answer. But still I felt that I was being watched, so I shrank back into my room.

When at first light the woman climbed up with berries for my breakfast, I asked had she slept sound through all the noise of the wolves. She hadn't heard a thing.

The next night I was ready for him.

> *Weave his shirt in one piece*
> *Polish his silver horn*
> *For he comes to bring ease*
> *To his lady all forlorn*

I had only just finished when his voice rose from the darkness. Will you come down to me? he asked.

I cannot. I'm afraid of waking the woman.

Is she your mother, that you fear to wake her?

No mother nor nothing to me, I said.

There was a long silence, so I thought he had gone. I was about to call out after him when he asked, more hoarsely, May I come up to you?

For a minute it seemed impossible, and then I remembered the rope. I knotted it round a sharp stone in the wall and threw it down, bracing myself for his weight.

The prince was all I had imagined. His hand grasping mine at the window was strong as a willow; his neck smelt of lavender, and the shirt on his back was clean as water. His voice was rough, but musical, and his lips against my cheek were soft as rabbits' whiskers. I laughed and tried to pull off his hunting gloves, but he held my hands still. I asked him, What do I sound like?

He said, I was so stirred by your song, I knew I would have no peace till I saw you.

I asked him, What do I look like?

He said, I was so moved by the sight of you at the window, I knew I would have no peace till I touched your face.

I tried to ask, What do I feel like?, but his mouth was stopping my mouth.

We were in accord by sunrise. If he heard me sing it was safe to call up to me. If he sounded the horn he wore in his belt I would climb down to him. If he brought me a gold ring I would give him my hand.

The next day, the woman brought me a basket of peas from her plot, and we shelled them together. She was snappish; she hadn't slept for the howling of the wolves. I nodded and shut my eyes to make a deeper darkness. I couldn't stop smiling.

What ails you today? she asked in her habitual whisper.

Nothing, I sang out. Nothing you need know, or maybe something you never will.

The bowl crashed against the wall; I could hear peas race across the stone. There is nothing I do not know, the woman bawled. Everything you think you know you have learned from me.

I tried to answer but she put her cold leathery hands over my eyes. You see nothing, she said; you are helpless as a lamb still wet from the ewe. Yet you have deceived me.

I bowed my head under the weight of her palms.

I have used up my years to keep you warm and fed, she said in my ear.

I answered, The fruits of the forest are free for all. I have given my days to keep you from loneliness.

The birds and the beasts are more faithful, she shouted. I have worn out my arms piling stone on stone because you begged me to keep you safe from the wind and the wolves and the hunting horn.

You should have known better than to give me what I asked for, I whispered, tears creeping down my face. Now the wind is scented with lavender, and the wolves howl because they cannot have him, and when he blows his royal horn, I will go to him.

There was a long silence. Nothing less royal, she said at last, smashing something down on the slab between us.

She guided my hand over the pieces of horn, common horn. The horn was mine, she said. I knew I would have no peace till I found you a prince. As she spoke her whisper deepened into a hoarse, musical voice, a voice I knew.

I pulled back and threw the sharp fragments in her face, calling her witch, monster, carrion, all the words she ever taught me.

When her footsteps had died away I heard the heavy bar fall across the door at the bottom of the tower. I waited till my pulse had stopped roaring. Not a sound. Did she mean to leave me to starve till I begged for forgiveness, she who had been the worst deceiver? I scrabbled in every corner of the room for my coil of rope, but she must have carried it away with her.

I wept into my hair. I wept enough to fill up another whole body, until the plaits grew heavy and matted. Weighing them between my hands, I realized that my hair was my own to do what I would with. The small paring knife was slow in my hand, but it sawed through the plaits one by one. I had never cut my hair before; I expected something like pain or blood, but all I felt was lightness, like a deer must feel at the shedding of antlers.

Knotted together, end by end, the plaits made the

strangest rope; it flowed over my hands like a giant snake. I speared it on a jagged stone and let myself out of the window. I was lightheaded, shivering, with nothing between me and the wolves but the paring knife in my belt. I walked to the edge of the clearing, hands out before me, till they met the first tree. A little way into the woods I came on some berries I recognized; they were sour but not poison. I wouldn't starve for all her rage.

I must have slept a little because when I woke it was night; silky blackness pressed on my eyelids. My face was scored by the bark of the tree I leaned on. Steps in the clearing; I stiffened. She was at the base of the tower, sobbing. Let me in, she called hoarsely. Let me climb up on your hair. Her voice was so deep, I had to remind myself that there was no prince.

I heard the puffs of breath as she began to climb. When she got to the top and looked in at the empty room, there was a wail like an animal in a trap, and then a sound like a hollow tree falling in the first storm of winter.

After several minutes had passed I edged forward. It was my left foot that found her. I felt my way along her body to her face; her eyes were shut, wet with what I thought was tears until I tasted it. I picked the thorns from her lids, as delicately as I could. Her hand came up and felt my head, the short damp hair. Can you see? I asked.

She whispered, What does it matter? The hedges may swell, the lavender may bloom, but it will all be wasteland when you're gone.

I took her head on my chest and wept over her, salt in her wounded eyes. It was the only way I knew to clean them. I didn't know whether they would heal, or whether she would have to learn the world from me now. We lay there, waiting to see what we would see.

There in the dark grass I asked,
Who were you
before you bought me for a handful of radishes?
And she said, Will I tell you my own story?
It is a tale of a brother.

VII

The Tale of the Brother

I HAVE NEVER been content to be nothing but a girl. And so I cannot tell you my story without that of my brother.

We were born on the same day; we shared our first breath. We grew up poor as tallow in a city you've never seen. The old people said if you stayed out all night you'd be found dead of cold in the morning. Like the other children in the orphanage, we had no people of our own; we were all we had.

My brother was not like other brothers. He showed me birds and beasts in the picture books and told me their names. He gave me his second-best ice pick and showed me how to fish through a hole. Sometimes he stayed out so late he had to throw pebbles with his blue fingers till I woke and opened the window for him to climb in.

I loved my brother, but sometimes I used to dream that when I woke up he would have been taken away without a trace. On that imagined morning, when I looked into the splinter of mirror over the hearth I would see his face in place of mine. Snow would be impatient outside the window like a dancer flinging off her veils. The old people would call me by my brother's name, let me tie his skates on, and send me out to the river with all the other boys. On that day, nothing and no one would stop me from skimming through the swarm of snow bees.

The day my brother was indeed taken away, I knew it was my fault for dreaming it.

He had already changed by then, or perhaps it was me. I couldn't be like him any more. The old people kept me indoors now, ever since my chest had started to swell as if stung. My brother poked me and laughed with a new cold face. He pushed away the picture books and ran out to the square, skates slung over his shoulder.

The reason I know what happened is that I followed him. I waited a while till the old people would have forgotten me, then I slid the latch. Fog came to meet me at the door. First I saw nothing, then the grey gauze shapes of houses. As I ran down the street the buildings thickened till I could believe in them. A perfect white coin slid from behind the clouds, and I wondered to see the moon up so early in the day, but then it brightened as if catching fire and I knew it was the sun, masked in fog.

Perhaps if it had been me who was skating through the square, it would have been me the woman took away with her. At first glance, squashed in bear skin, I must have looked like a boy, or near enough. I was standing at the corner, trying to distinguish my brother in the swirl of skaters, when she drove by with the bells tinkling on her white sleigh. Slush spattered my boots. I was near enough to see her face, lean, knowledgeable, too cold to need beauty. I was not so far away that I couldn't glimpse my brother's tousled head buried in her ermine. I came that close.

I didn't shout out. I stood like a tree stump, rooted in dirty snow. The sleigh bells faded in the distance.

That night I didn't sleep. Ice blossomed on the windows till they grew dark.

The next morning my face in the mirror was the same as ever, the face of a girl, square with freckles like a spray of mud. When the old people asked me where my brother was gone, I said, A woman in white furs took him away.

They slapped me across the mouth and told me not to make up stories. They said every boy comes home when he's good and hungry.

When they asked me the same question a few days later, I said I didn't know. They didn't ask me again after that. I suppose they thought he had drowned in a hole in the river. They gave me some red shoes, nearly new, but they never spoke his name.

I went down to the river with a net on a stick and caught a little fish. I left it on my brother's bed, in case he came back, but the new boy who moved into that bed that night had eaten it by morning. I lay awake after the others were asleep, listening for the faintest pebble, but nothing shook the window except snow and wind. I pulled a feather out of the old pillow and breathed on it to conjure up a bird that would carry me off, but it only grew damp.

I shut my eyes and was my brother, riding along in the furs at the bottom of the sleigh in a hot sleep, dreaming only of dinner. Snow hissed under the runners, crows screamed overhead, wolves complained in the nearby trees, but my brother lay curled up like a cat at the woman's feet.

I woke up cursing, words I didn't know I knew. Who was she? How dare she? Had she no brother of her own, that she had to steal mine? My face was wet, as if it had started to thaw in the night.

I put on my new scarlet shoes that my brother had never seen and set off to find him. I looked back three times but no one followed.

That day and the next and the next I searched the city, a street at a time. I saw boys of all sorts, big and small, boys with skates and boys with clogs, boys on errands and boys out for mischief, boys who lent me their spinning tops and boys who pinched me and boys who didn't see me, but none of them was my brother. At night I hid in stables beside the steaming straw. An old woman gave me a fish tail once, and a bread man let me have a stale loaf another day. When snow fell I hunkered under the eaves of an inn, smelling the fire. Afterwards I couldn't tell the white streets apart, or whether I had searched them before. I was walking in circles so cold I couldn't remember my name.

In my dreams the sleigh went faster and faster till it was flying above the trees. It was not fur I was lying in but feathers, the plumage of a swan big enough to fly to the edge of the world.

While I was asleep a girl tried to steal my shoes. I woke as she was unbuckling the second strap with nimble fingers. I seized her wrists and hit her on the nose like my brother taught me. She spat blood, red as sunset over the straw-flecked snow. She laughed and laughed.

When I had fastened my shoes on again I let the thief come into the straw beside me. She gave out plenty of heat for her size. Her tales were tall but they warmed my ears. She showed me her knife and said how she could get any pair of shoes if she wanted. She told me how she'd never known any home but a stable, nor eaten a bite but what her fingers filched from a stall. How when she was grown she'd have a great house and a gleaming sleigh to carry her back and forth across the city.

I told her about my brother, to stop her boasting, because a brother was better than all these things that could be stolen. And then I remembered how I had lost him. She asked where he was and hot tears ran down my face on to hers.

In the morning she led me back to the great square. If they were here once they'll be here again, she said; a thief is always drawn back like a leaf to a drain. She stole a hot pastry and broke a piece off for me before disappearing down a side street.

All that day I waited, slamming my feet up and down to warm them. Sun was such a dazzle it hurt my eyes;

iced puddles winked at me as if they knew my business. I kept my eyes shut until I heard bells coming, but it was only some boys on a homemade sled. I called out to them to see if they remembered my brother, but they answered with a snowball. It missed. I stood still and kept my eyes shut till I thought they'd frozen over.

Much later it was dark between the houses. My skates had grown into the ground, my mittens were stuck to my coat. I wouldn't go back to the stable tonight. I would stay there in the emptying square until I couldn't feel anything at all. They would find me in the morning, a new statue for the city. More like a bear cub than an ice maiden, but still, something worth pointing at.

Sudden as thunder the sleigh came round the corner. Before I saw her pale face I knew it was the one. White fur and bells passing me, and with a lurch I had thrown myself forward and grasped the end of the sleigh. I was skidding through the streets, slush spraying me to the hips, dragged along like a feather.

It seemed an hour before the sleigh made a sharp turn and I was thrown into a ditch. With stiff arms I wiped the snow from my face. It was clean, tasting of nothing. I had never been into the country before. I got to my feet and peered after the sleigh. Bells hung fainter on the air. Darkness thickened between tall trees. I was lost.

So as to keep moving as long as I could, I plodded down the road. I could feel nothing below the knees; I was like that beggar girl with wooden legs I saw in the market once. Only when I caught sight of my fingers, hanging like slaughterhouse rags, did I realize that I had lost my mittens.

Just when the dark seemed to be wrapping me round, and I was thinking of lying down in the snow, a light pricked its way through the trees. I was walking like a drunk by now; sometimes the light disappeared or I thought I was only imagining it. But at last the path turned a corner, and I with it, and there in front of me was the biggest house I had ever seen. A lantern hung at the door, shining on the empty sleigh.

What I did next was not like the girl I had been. I climbed the steps, stiff-kneed. When my hands failed to make any sound on the door but a feeble patting, I pulled off my shoes, their red leather soaked almost black, and swung at the wood with their hard heels. Open up, I bellowed. Open up this minute. I have come for my brother.

When she opened the door I was distracted for a second by her face, whiter than the fur of her collar.

But then I remembered, and flung my shoes at her feet. She stepped back. Take my red shoes, I shouted, but give me back my brother.

There he was in the hall, peering round her skirt. His mouth was full of cake; his grin caught the light.

Why him? I howled like a baby. Why him and not me?

Her smile was gentler than I could ever have expected. She opened her arms as wide as they would go and said, Come in, come in.

After I had eaten my fill I asked,
Who were you
before you stole my brother?
And she said, Will I tell you my own story?
It is a tale of a spinster.

VIII

The Tale of the Spinster

YOUR FACE IS no fortune, so elbowgrease must be your dowry. That's what my mother always said to me. It was her best joke, one she liked to repeat to passers-by.

Once she caught me asleep when I should have been carding wool, and she pricked my shame all over my face with the comb. I never idled again. What I needed ever after I worked for, or borrowed at interest, or did without. I am as rich now as I was once poor, and half as rich as I am lonely. If I have turned to theft at last, it is because I was once robbed of the best thing I had, and the worst of it all is that I deserved to lose it.

It all began with a boast. My mother's mouth was too big for her stomach; she could talk up a storm at the first drop of rain. My daughter can spin anything, she would bawl out of the window at hesitant customers; wool, cotton, hemp, flax, nothing is beyond her. Come this way to the widow's daughter, the best spinster in this city or any.

For all her talk, I knew she despised me. I saw her biting on her brass ring; I could count her rages by knots in the thread I showed her at the end of each day. But the more I disappointed her, the more custom she drummed up at her window.

All went well as long as she oversaw the spinning herself; her hands spotted multitudes of sins and saw to them as quick as fleas. But with the passing of years my mother's fingers began to curl. Her hands dragged themselves around the house like stiff spiders. After the smashing of the third milk jug, she resigned herself to sitting all day at the window. She stared at her traitor knuckles and harangued any buyer who went to any other door than ours.

Inside her she began to spin gall into sickness; by the end of a year it swelled as big as a baby.

In her final fever, she took to screaming a single phrase over and over, as if they could hear her throughout the city: Shit into gold! My daughter can spin shit into gold! But her eyes followed me around the hearth. They hung on my slippery spinning wheel.

On her last morning, my mother's hands reached out, scrabbling for a purchase. Not knowing what to give her, I put my hands in hers. She held on, her long nails scoring my palms. The clouds in her eyes parted; her voice was sane. Daughter, she said, if I have trodden you underfoot it was to wash out the dirt. If I have trampled you, it was to mesh your fibres into something useful. She tugged at the brass ring on her little finger until it came off, edged with blood; she slid it on to mine. Work will be your mother, she whispered; it will lead you through dark days; it will clear you a level place to rest at last.

I sat quite still for more than an hour, listening to the silence, feeling the air between my lips. Then I prised my mother's cold fingers off mine and stood up.

Sympathy for my loss brought in twice as many orders. The room began to fill up with bales. Whenever I grew drowsy over the wheel, hypnotized by spinning sunlight, my mother's ghostly croak startled my ear. Whenever I wanted to shut the door and hide away, my mother's foot wedged it open. Whenever I tried to refuse an order, my mother's hand closed around my throat. Flax mounted higher than my head on every side, and sealed off the window. I sat like a prisoner, and knew that I could never spin it all if I lived to be a hundred years old.

I began to look around for an assistant. Some were too slow, others too slapdash. This one was a chatterer; that one smelt sour. Finally I heard of a young woman who had been spinning all her life until her house had burned down around her. If she was burned into charcoal, I didn't care. Be she flat-footed from treading, stung-lipped from licking, swollen-thumbed from pressing the thread, I would take her.

She was none of these things. She was small like a robin and slow in the head; sentences seemed too much for her. I showed her my room, walled with glowing flax. She stood on one foot and said, in her halting way, that she was thinking of going back to the land of her birth. I gave her my most pleading smile and called her Little Sister. She seemed to like the name. How would she take her pay? Cloth or plate or coin?

She didn't seem to follow. Let me sit at table? she asked.

Gladly.

Eat from plate drink from cup?

I would feed her with my own hands if only she would spin my trouble away.

She agreed to stay until the room was empty. I watched, wide-eyed, as she ate through the work, hour by hour, day by day. I sat at the window and called merrily to passing customers. I shared plate and cup with her every evening.

The day Little Sister cleared the last corner, a new load arrived, more than ever before. She chewed her lip and said she wanted to go back to the land of her birth.

I put my hands together and begged. How could I reward her? Dresses or bracelets or milky pearls?

She shook her head as if she didn't understand the words. Let me sleep in bed? she asked.

Willingly.

Be sister truly and you not shamed?

I would join my blood to hers for life if only she would spin me right-way-up again.

She agreed to stay until the room was empty. My eyes rested on her as she cut through the work; every day there was another shaft of light across the room. I sat at the window in my best dress and exchanged greetings with handsome merchants. I shared pillow and blanket with Little Sister every night; she snored, but not loud enough to keep me awake. The day she cleared the last corner, a huge load of flax arrived from the richest weaver. It filled all the room except for a circle around her wheel and stool. She bit her thumb and said she was going back to the land of her birth, and this time she sounded like she meant it.

I went down on my knees and put my face to the dusty floor. Threads clung in my hair as I looked at her. How could I make it up to her, if she stayed? Would she take half my house, half my fortune, the ring off my finger?

She shook her head so slowly it seemed as if she was searching for something in the corners of the room. Flesh of your flesh? she mumbled.

What?

First-born in my arms?

I put my head back to laugh, and told her she was welcome to a whole litter of my future offspring, if only she would spin me out of this mess.

She agreed to stay.

Until the room is empty? I asked, making sure.

Stay, she repeated. Stay always.

Nothing could have made me happier. With Little Sister at home, spinning up her magic, I could go out again, feel the sun pinking my face. I dressed even richer than I was and paid calls on fine ladies, dined with weavers, drank with moneymen. Not that I was idling: everything I did was for the sake of business; each courtesy to a merchant, an arrow aimed true. And, finding my vocation, I learned that my mother was right after all. Work was a rope on a ship in rough water, a candle on a creaking staircase, a potato in a beggar's embers. It kept me sane and bright-eyed; it kept me from dwelling on the past; it even kept me from remembering that I was a woman.

Which is the only clue I can give as to how I, so sensible, daughter to a far-seeing mother, found myself with child.

I'd have died before telling the merchant in question, turning up like a beggar at his door. I wouldn't have married even if I could have; I was a woman of business now, a woman of affairs, far too far gone to make a good wife. I threw up my breakfast every day for a week. Little Sister found me weeping into a pile of flax, and knelt down beside me.

We worked it all out. It would be winter by the time I grew fat, so I could wear a cloak that hid everything. I would tell the neighbours that my assistant had got herself a great belly. (Too dull in the wits to shout out for help, poor creature.) I would boast of my kindness in keeping her on. (We working women must stand by each other.) Little Sister could keep an eye on the baby while she spun, the thread whirring soothingly on to the bobbin.

I should have known things wouldn't run that smoothly. The night of my confinement I lay gnawing at the sheets, squeezing Little Sister's hand whenever I needed to scream, so she would scream in her own voice for the neighbours to hear. It seemed to me in my delirium that my mother had tied my thighs together, so the shame would split me apart.

It felt like many days later when Little Sister lifted the bawling gout of flesh in her thread-scarred hands. I cut the cord myself, I was in such a hurry. He's all yours, I said, trying to laugh.

She took him away to be christened. I pressed my face into the soaked sheet and thought of being dead.

As soon as the bleeding had stopped I returned to work. I flattered buyers, traded witticisms with weavers, made it my business to know the name of every merchant's wife in the city. I was thin again, fast on my feet, to be seen around town in every house but my own.

Because the baby cried all day, all night. Little Sister claimed he hated flax; it made him sneeze. I nodded, but knew he was a thing possessed. I had bales of flax stacked higher around the four walls to muffle his bawling. The spinning was suffering too: Little Sister was always running to see what was the matter with him. It grew hotter; the thread smelt of him. I stayed out of their way as much as I could, but one afternoon I came home to find Little Sister asleep over her wheel, and the baby drooling into a fresh hank of wool. I picked it up and slapped him across the face.

Little Sister woke at the baby's first shriek, but said nothing. I walked out of the door and stayed away till the following evening. By the time I came back everything seemed peaceful. Outside the door were stacks of butter-coloured bobbins, ready for collection. Inside was nothing at all. The room was absolutely empty.

I ran faster than I ever had before, faster than my mother would have thought decent, faster than I thought I could. I caught up with them at last, on the bridge just outside the city gates. Little Sister had bound the baby into her dress; he was fast asleep against her flesh.

Gasping for breath, I told her to give back what was mine. She looked me in the eye like she never had before and said, You promised. First-born.

I begged her, for friendship, for sisterhood, to take all the gold I had but give me back my child. She curled her lip and said, Your gold not worth shit.

I knelt down on the cold stone of the bridge and clung to her skirts. Don't desert me, Little Sister. I'll be different.

She looked at me with something like pity and said, Don't know me.

What?

Never asked my name.

Didn't I?

Never boy's name neither, she told me. Taking him away now so he know who.

She waited till my eyes fell, then walked. My knees felt frozen to the ground. I looked through the slots in the parapet. The black river was sliding towards me, bringing who knew how many hardworking days, who knew which desires, which regrets.

I stumbled along the bridge, caught her sleeve and asked,
Who were you
before you became Little Sister?
And she said, Tell you story?
Tale of cottage.

IX

The Tale of the Cottage

I ONCE HAD brother that mother say we were pair of hands one fast one slow. I once had father he got lost in woods. I once had mother.

Huntman had wonderful beard. Let me and brother come too into woods with gun. Brother let me help little house of branches till broke and he push away.

Things changed after we held broom behind our hut and they jumped. Things went sour milk in churn all forgotten. Sky went far off and leaves went scrish scrish. Too cold for snow, say mother. Put brother and me sleeping with chickens not annoy huntman.

One night hit her harder whap whap so her voice went big into rafters woke chickens say, Curse you.

Then on no luck for huntman. Means no meat for us. Brother say mother eat her words. I see only nuts and old bread. She say, Sorry sorry. She put last drops holy water on huntman gun. Still no luck. One night he come home snowed like pine. Next day lie in smelly furs all day bellyache. Bang fist on wall call angels witness. Say, How can we feed your children when we can't even feed ourselves?

Moonrise I holding chicken for warm hear him through wall. They talking small not like whap whap. She say, It's their home. He say, What's a home with a bare table?

Later after sounds like running I hear him say, Pick one. You can't feed two birds with a single stone. The little one's no earthly use not right in the head.

After mother cry and gone quiet like sleeping I hold my head like apple shake it for see what sick. Sound all right. Never can tell.

Morning huntman let us come too into woods for rabbits brother and me. I dance like appledust. Trees come thicker round till no sky left. He tell brother go look at snare. He sit me behind tree for game. Make little fire give bread say, No sound good girl.

I suck bread soft and wait for them come back. Cold. Sound like crows. Good girl. Want home. Cry.

Lots hours later fire gone small. Hear feet think maybe lost father coming with acorn teeth and ivy where eyes were. Try run fall on root.

Brother it was whistling. I call out. Don't cry little nut I found you I'll bring you home, he say. Twice as old and ten times as clever. I put legs round waist and hold on.

Hut shine light. I feared. Stop at door. Seem like dark inside. Brother say, Home again little hen. Lift latch mother cry cry like happy. Huntman angered say, Why did you get yourself lost you halfwit girl? He not remember game. No food on table. Mother face wet salty.

Night they talking low again. Brother sleeping. I push nosy chicken away put ear on wall. Huntman say, You want to watch them starve? You want to wait till the cramps buckle them up? Mother cry Nonononono like punched out. He soft voice now say, Don't take on so woman. Don't fight fate. You can have more when times are good again.

I think of having more more food more fire more shoes till sleep.

Morning mother not get up. I want into furs with. Huntman say, Woods again today.

Walk lots hours. Where trees thickest he make small fire say, Rest now like good children while I go deeper in to chop wood for a while.

Brother want go with. Huntman say, Look after your sister or I'll beat the skin off you.

We wait. Lots hours later trees so thick no light at all outside fire. Sound like wolves. Fire tiny. Brother go for wood. I cry so he come back curl round me. Warm fart. Then no fire. He say, Don't worry half pint I'll bring you home as soon as it gets light.

Wake all covered snow cold laughing. Throw ball brother. Home home home like song loud through snow. When brother wake face like old bread. Say he can't find way when all white. I say, Follow me dance like snow home to mother.

Snow thicker feels like no feet no hands no noses. Brother follow me cry try hide it.

Get dark again. Brother go up tree see wide round. Slither down say, There's a light, little loaf.

We walk walk walk. When ground dip all dark again I not cry. I not cry. Brother find light again.

When we see up close dazzle I think morning. When we see cottage I think dreaming. Windows shine like sugar walls brown like gingerbread.

Brother say, Home. Not home. Then brother say, Come. I feared. I known wormy apples with shiny skin. I seen rotted teeth behind handsome beard. Brother go knock knock.

When door open I think mother then no. Young. Woman say, What brought you here? No words from brother no words from me. Woman say, Stop here with me tonight and no harm will touch you.

Bed so soft I think hot snow.

She wake me blowing on nose. I tell her walls gingerbread. She say, And the door is toffee and the chimney is liquorice and the beds are chocolate. I not know words. Laugh anyway. She make pancakes two each me her and brother. Her eyes red like crying. Face smooth like girl.

We can stay if work. She know all that grow in woods. She know how talk rabbits into big cage in kitchen so never starving. Brother chop logs laugh like grown man ask kiss get slap. She teach me roll dough for baking into shapes of woman tree star.

Only bad nights. Wrap round brother like bread before oven. Very quiet say home like would get me there.

One night brother gone out bed. I look sugar crystal window. No steps in moon snow all swallowed up. Too feared to cry. Then woman scream like mother old nightmares say, Get out of my bed. Brother fall on floor. Say, Just for a warm. She hit something. Brother say, Lonely.

Morning woman wake me stroking say, Bonny red cheeks what will we do? I look brother out axing wood. Bake bread, say I. She laughing.

Days on days go by snow shrinks to nothing. I dance like white flowers pushing through cold head first. Brother has hair chin instead of smile. Woman make him chop all trees died in winter till hands red like robins. I pick mouldy seeds from good.

One day we baking brother walk in call her name I never heard lift her skirt behind. Woman no scream this time. Put skinning knife to chin make drop of blood till he get in rabbit cage. He laughing as she chain it. I laughing I feared. He shake cage. It hold fast.

Night I cold so woman let me in with her. Make like she not hear brother shouting. I say, He cold. She say, Not for long.

I sleep warm between arms. Wake up understanding she go to skin him like rabbit.

Slip into kitchen heart banging like churn. Brother sleep till I find key in drawer open chain put hand over mouth.

He climb out stretching. Come on, he whisper. You're safe with me little nut.

Not safe anywhere.

He shake my head to wake it. Don't you understand? Now the snow is gone I can find our way home to mother.

No, I crying quiet. Home not home if mother not mother.

But you can't stay here, she's mad, she's got a knife.

Take my chances, I say.

He look for long while then nod. I give him fresh bake loaf shape like me. Tell him no come back with huntman gun. No come back ever.

I watch him run through trees. Snow begin falling cover tracks. I lean head in door wait for woman to wake.

Snow melting round next morning I ask,
Who you before so angry?
And she say, Will I tell you my own story?
It is a tale of a skin.

X

The Tale of the Skin

S EE THIS LEAF, little girl, blackened under the snow? It has died so it will be born again on the branch in springtime. Once I was a stupid girl; now I am an angry woman. Sometimes you must shed your skin to save it.

There was a king, there was a queen. He was as rich as she was beautiful. They were as good as they were happy. They lived in a palace on the edge of a vast forest where the leaves never fell. They were wrapped up in each other like a nut in its shell.

The only strange thing about this king was that his favourite, of all the splendid beasts that snorted and tossed their heads in his stables, was a donkey with lopsided ears. The princess was allowed to stroke the creature's ears on feast days, but never to ride her.

When I say the princess, I suppose I am referring to

myself, though I have come such a long way from that little girl that I can hardly recognize her. I remember that I had golden hair, lily cheeks and ruby lips, just like my mother. I know I used to run in the garden and muddy my ankles. I liked to slip out of the palace grounds and visit a cottage in the evergreen forest. An old woman lived there who earned her bread by her needle, and by gathering herbs for medicines. I used to call her my flower-woman because her face was dry like a flower pressed in a book.

When the queen took sick, as good queens do, the king sent for physicians from east and west, far and wide. I overheard the maids talking about it. I asked to look at my mother but they told me to go and play.

By the time the physicians arrived, through the first drifts of snow, she was past hope. My father's knees were planted at her bedside like pine trees. I saw him through a crack in the door.

Snow fell on the palace like a shroud that night, and in the spring the lilies stood tall on her grave. The king was still locking himself away every day to lament. He had his favourite donkey brought to him, and wept into her hide until it was soaked; he slept between the animal's legs each night. His courtiers breathed through their mouths.

Fearing his mind was disturbed, they urged him to find a new wife. For the sake of his subjects, for the sake of the princess, for his own sweet sake. He shook his head from side to side as if to shake grief loose. No one could compare to his queen, be bellowed at them: where would he find again such golden hair, such lily cheeks, such ruby lips?

Finally he let them bring in the portraits. He stared at Flemish princesses and Spanish infantas, English duchesses and even an empress from beyond the sea. But though one had yellow hair and another white cheeks and another red lips, not one of them had all these at once, so the king smashed each picture in turn against the walls of his room. The donkey brayed in panic, and stove in the side of the throne with her hoofs. The king tore the hair from one canvas, the cheeks from a second, the lips from a third, and squeezed them together in his hand.

The mingled howls of man and beast travelled along the corridors. The cowering courtiers held perfumed handkerchiefs to their noses so as not to catch the king's madness. His food was set on a gold tray outside his door.

After the death of my mother, I grew paler and taller. My curves prickled as they swelled; my limbs hurt from stretching. Not all the flower-woman's herbs could make me sleep through the night. One day I was walking through the palace when I heard a moan. I stared at the door and remembered that the king was my father. I picked up the heavy gold tray and brought it into him.

The king was as hairy and grimy as the donkey asleep beside him. He looked up as if the heavens had opened.

I cleared my throat. Here is your dinner.

He peered closer. To think that all this time, the answer was under my nose, he whispered.

I gave him a doubtful smile.

Tell me, do you love me?

Of course.

The words barely had time to leave my mouth. I have been waiting too long, cried my father, and then he dashed the tray from my hand and pressed his mouth to mine. Bowls spun like snow, goblets shattered like hail. I knew that something was very wrong. He pleated me along the length of his body in a way no one had ever done before. He held me at arm's length and said, Such ruby lips, such lily cheeks, such golden hair is all my heart desires. You will be mine again, and more than ever before.

By the time I got out of the room, my dress was torn in three places. I smelt of dirt, and fear, and something I didn't understand. I wrapped myself in a cloak and ran to the flower-woman's cottage.

The courtiers had it proclaimed that the king's mind was unhinged; in a sort of waking dream he thought himself to be young again and the princess to be her mother in virgin form; a natural mistake. They urged me to stall, to let him court me while they sent for better physicians from farther afield; it could do the poor man no harm. They spoke of compassion, but I knew they were terrified.

Each afternoon I would be called to the king's chamber, with a maid for a chaperone. Some days he called me daughter; others, lover; others, his beauty. He sometimes let me comb the lice from his hair. His starving lips would make their way from the tips of my fingers to the crease at my elbow. He would serenade me on his knees, fawn over my forehead and weep in my lap. His words, sometimes in languages I had never heard, filled up the room till I couldn't breathe.

So matters continued for a month. If I loved him, the king whimpered, why would I not lie down in his bed? The courtiers insisted that I continue to humour him. The flower-woman told me how to win myself a little time. I had never played the petulant princess, but I set my mind to it now.

I told him, You have torn my dress. I need another before I marry you; would you take me for a beggar? I will have one as gold as the sun.

The king laughed out loud. He sent his courtiers to inquire through the whole kingdom. The only needle that could make such a dress belonged to the flower-woman. She worked with such meticulous detail that another moon passed, and I was still safe.

On the day the gold dress was finished, I put it on and danced a waltz for the king. The donkey brayed in time with the music. But when he would have let down my hair, I backed away and told him, I need another dress before I marry you; would you take me for a vagabond? I will have one as silver as the moon.

The king clapped his hands. He sent his courtiers back to the flower-woman. She worked with such tender care that another two moons passed, and I was still safe.

On the day the silver dress was finished, I put it on and danced a polka for the king. The donkey flapped her lopsided ears in time. But when he would have seized me in his arms, I backed away and told him, I need another dress before I marry you; would you take me for a woman of the roads? I will have one as glittering as the stars.

The king caused a fanfare to be blown. He sent his courtiers back to the flower-woman. She worked with such infinite slowness that another three moons passed, and I was still safe.

On the day the glittering dress was finished, I put it on and danced a mazurka for the king. But when he would have lifted my skirt, I backed away. I had one last request, and then I would marry him. Give me a cloak, I said, made of the hide of this donkey.

His face fell into itself, crumbled like a rotten pine cone. I almost softened.

Winter is tightening its grip on the palace, I cried. Would you have me colder than this dumb beast? Would you grudge me what the least of your brute subjects wears? Would you have me go naked against the wind?

My father hung his head.

I wept into my pillow that night, from relief. The kingdom might be turned upside down, but I would be safe now. I listened to the far-off scream of the wind.

The king came to my room at first light, and spread the skin before me, still warm with blood. His grin hung in folds as he said, Tomorrow shall be our wedding.

All that day I stayed in my room. I clung to the blanket and said to myself, You're a grown girl now. Worse things happen in the stories. There must be worse husbands. He is not a goblin, or a bear, or a monster. He is only your father, and mad.

And then I shuddered and thought to myself, He could kill me. I belong to him as surely as that donkey did. He could skin me like he has skinned his beloved beast, and who could stop him? I bent my head and wept until the blanket ran with rain.

But my old flower-woman came to me in the night, as I lay awake. You must fly now, she whispered, alone, in disguise, into some distant land where no one knows your name. She blackened with soot that cursed golden hair, those lily cheeks and ruby lips; she showed me how to rub dirt under my nails. I took my three bright dresses, my mother's wedding ring, and the donkey skin, wrapped round me to ward off curious glances.

It smelt of blood and shit, but it kept me warm. Lying curled up in ditches and caves, night after night, I hoped the predators would take me for a rotten carcass. The stars looked down on me and laughed. Was this freedom? I wondered. Was this better than a throne?

As I drifted from my father's kingdom into the next, following the caravan of days, I shed every layer of pride. Hair began to grow in unexpected places. It hung about my face like a thorn-bush; seeds and insects clung to my head. I began to learn the lessons of the ass. Eat anything that doesn't move. Snatch any warmth going. Suffer and endure.

I kept moving only because I had nowhere to stay. Children in tiny villages threw old boots at my head, called me Stinking Donkeyskin. I lived on what I begged or stole. I had meant to sell my dresses, but I found I couldn't part with them; they were the only brightness I had left. The first month of winter, my shoes felt like iron; by the third, they had worn out. I didn't notice losing them on the road at last; my feet were as hard as the scraps of shoe leather by the time they slid off. I had never felt so ugly, or so faint, or so strong.

I had lost count of the moons by the time I came to a strange kingdom where the trees were not green. The first time I saw the turning of the leaves it bewildered me; I thought it might be the end of the world. Not even the flower-woman could make a dress as bright as this destruction. I thought some invisible fire must be burning each leaf from the outside in; I could see the green veins retreating before the crisp tide of flame. When leaves fell on me I staggered out of their way. More colours than I had names for covered my feet as I walked. At night I slept on piles of crackling leaves, strangely comforted that all things were sharing in my fall.

My last night of vagabondage, or freedom, felt like any other. I curled up in a hollow tree to keep out of the wind. I was woken at dawn by the jangle of the hunt. Catch it alive if you can, came the cry. The dogs had sniffed me out. The huntsmen wept with laughter when I limped into the light. They carried me through the crackling forest, over the river, as a living trophy for their prince.

Now I was back in the land of the living, I could smell my own lowliness. Who are you? asked the prince, glancing up from his leather-bound book.

A poor donkey without mother or father.

What are you good for?

Nothing but to have boots thrown at my head.

He was the most handsome man I had ever seen. He seemed amused by my answers, and rewarded me with a corner in the kitchen. In return for washing dish-cloths, peeling turnips and raking ashes, I had the right to sleep. The animal in me was glad of the fire, but I hated to hear the heavy bolt slide home, last thing at night. The turn-spits joked so coarsely I could barely understand them. One of them with a face like a cabbage tried to find out what was behind that hairy hide of mine, but I brayed like a mad donkey and he backed away.

At last it was spring, and the air softened. There came a feast day when I was released from my duties. I wandered through the empty kitchen after dinner. A round-bellied copper pot hung on the wall; I caught sight of my own face in it, and flinched.

Down by the river I dropped my heavy skin and rinsed the past away. The comb hurt me but I was glad of its teeth. My mother's wedding ring slid easily on to my thin finger. I drew the golden dress from my pack, shook out its creases, and danced for my own reflection till it seemed the sun had come up twice. Next I tried the silver dress, spinning to make the birds think it was moonrise. Finally I slipped over my head the dress that glittered like the stars. Even without looking I knew myself to be beautiful. My fair hair flowed bright as the river. I was a princess again, right down to my slim toes in their shining slippers. From the castle, music enticed my footsteps.

No one challenged me when I entered the ballroom:

the dress's magic opened every door. The prince followed me with his disbelieving eyes, and asked me to dance, three times in a row. It seems to me that we have met before, he said, but I only twirled faster. There is something so oddly familiar about you, he said, and yet you are unique, a swan among these common ducks.

I laughed, and began to tell him stories of my own kingdom. It was like a miracle to be speaking aloud again, to say more than three words at a time.

I slipped away when he wasn't looking. Down by the river I dressed myself in rags again and muddied my face and nails. I couldn't stop smiling.

The next day I expected to be the last of my time of trial. With a light heart I threw bones to the dogs and scrubbed fat from the floor; behind my donkey skin I walked like a queen. I knew the prince must be searching every room, every inch of the castle, for his missing beauty. The kitchen was bubbling over with gossip about the stranger's golden hair, lily cheeks and ruby lips. I knew exactly what would happen; my ears were pricked for the royal step on the stair.

It was evening by the time the courtiers reached the bottom of the castle. I had gravy and flour on my cheeks, but fanfares in my heart. I did not even look up as the royal party made their way through the kitchens, lifting their robes above the dirt. As I knew he would, the prince stopped and said, Come here, girl.

His eyes must have fallen on my mother's wedding ring, a thick band of gold that no amount of soot could hide. I looked up at him with a hint of amusement.

Who are you?

A poor donkey, I repeated.

What brought you into this kingdom?

Fear and need.

He was staring now, as if trying to see past the layer of grime. I smiled, to make it even easier for him. My features had not changed since yesterday; my voice was as sweet as ever, if he could only hear it. Inside my head I said, Look at me. Make me beautiful in your beholding.

The prince's eyes narrowed.

Was he drugged, that he couldn't hear my heart calling to his? Surely he would know me all at once, any minute now, and burst out laughing at the absurdity of all such disguises?

He shook his head, as if collecting his wits, and turned back to his courtiers.

Was I tempted to cry out, to declare myself? It never seemed to me, thinking about it afterwards, that there had been any chance, any time, anything worth saying.

I listened as courtiers ascended the stairs, discussing to which kingdoms their prince should send messengers in search of the mysterious princess. I swayed yet stood. When everyone else had finished their work and left the kitchen, I remained, a hollow tree refusing to fall.

My ring I dropped in the royal soup bowl for him to choke on. The gold and silver and starry dresses I left scattered by the river; let him think his lost beauty drowned. The donkey skin I pulled tightly around me as I set out for home.

Not on the whole length of my journey would I see any man half so handsome. Through the long nights in ditches and hollow trees I could not help thinking of him. I knew by now he would be sickening for love. The physicians would be ordering the cooks to prepare rare delicacies, but all in vain.

If he guessed his mistake, if he wanted me back, I thought, let him suffer and work for it as I had worked and suffered. Let him follow me over a mountain of iron and a lake of glass, and wear out three swords in my defence. But at my truest, lying awake trying to count the stars, I knew my prince would not follow. In my mind's eye I saw him in his palace, stroking the gold and silver and starry dresses which were fading now like leaves in winter, weeping for a spotless princess who did not exist, who had drowned in the river of time.

The king I had once called father had died childless and frothing, I learned over a beggars' camp-fire. The throne was now occupied by a distant cousin.

The flower-woman was standing outside my cottage that winter day, as if expecting me. She was a little older, but still smiling.

She gave me a drink to clear my head; she washed me in scented water; she put on me a new dress of homespun wool. She took me to the king's grave; there we spread the donkey skin, cracked and frayed. I didn't need it any longer; let it keep him warm.

These were my feet, balancing like a cat's. This was my hand, the colour of a rose. I looked down and recognized myself.

There by the graveside I asked,
Who were you
before you learned how to make dresses?
And the flower-woman said, Will I tell you my own story?
It is a tale of a needle.

XI

The Tale of the Needle

WHEN I WAS the age that you are now, I had never done an hour's work. There was nothing I knew how to make or mend. I was innocent of all effort; I was blank as a page.

As a child in my parents' manor I used to play a game because I knew no better. I would walk into the kitchens ten minutes before dinner and lift my little hand. Stop, I would call at the top of my voice. And they always did. How well the turn-spit made a gargoyle of himself; how carefully the cook stilled the ladle half-way to his lips; how obediently the maid held the soup tureen until her face grew scarlet. Only when I clicked my fingers might the servants slump into ordinary life again, like grumbling giants woken from their sleep of ages. I had many games, but that one was the best.

They had no choice: the turn-spit and the cook and the maid. My father always told them his little beauty was never to be crossed. My mother said no one was ever to make her baby cry.

You see, before they had me they were both so old they thought for sure they were barren. They swore complicated vows, swallowed medicines made from boiled frogs, and went on pilgrimages for months at a time. At last, like a gift from above, my mother grew big, and my father put a chicken in the pot of every family on our estate. The day I was born they lifted me into my father's hands, and he roared out so all could hear: This is my beloved daughter, in whom I am well pleased.

From the very first day of life I wore gold mesh gloves so that nothing would ever soil my fingers. When I was a baby, they told me, I used to try to tear them off, but soon I grew placid and laid my hands across my belly like jewelled fans. For many years I didn't learn to walk, because I was carried everywhere – not by my parents, who had grown frail, but by the most sure-footed of the servants. Grateful fireworks erupted every month on the date of my birth.

The only lesson I had to learn was the list of my virtues: how my face was the fairest, my wit the sharpest, my heart the most angelic, my singing the most comparable to a lark's in all the land. Everyone who set eyes on me fell in love with me, I was told.

And I believed every word of it. Why would they have said it unless it was true?

I was content, I suppose, though having no basis for comparison I couldn't be sure. It felt more like sleep than joy. The manor had a drowsy air to it. Even the fire seemed lazy as it ate away at the logs. Whenever I asked a question that began with why, I would be told that things were done just as they had always been done for a hundred years before. What reason could there be to change?

Our manor was surrounded by a wide ring of gardens, in which something was always in flower and something else in fruit. Beyond that stood a huge bramble hedge, its blades so thickly knitted that when I stood near it I could see only chinks of blue light from the outside world. No one ever went outside if they could help it. Hadn't we everything we needed here?

About this time I was becoming restless. The year before and every year before that I had been peaceful, but this year I was growing, my fingers lengthening and straining against their gold nets. As the childish lines of my body were forced into curves, my mind began to writhe; it was as if some unseen hand was nudging me, magicking me into a shape that was not my own. I kept asking for a kitten of my own to play with, even though my parents always said it might hurt me. Poisonous feelings rushed through me with no warning. Greed, when there was nothing I lacked. Anger, when I had nothing to resent. Despair, when I was the luckiest girl in the world.

I thought I knew every room in the castle, having spent my childhood wandering up and down its many staircases, taking the freedom of each scullery, gallery or bedchamber. But one day I was out in the rose garden playing with my golden hoop for lack of anything else to do when I looked back at the tall grey tower and realized that I had never been up there. No door was locked against me, but I had never found a staircase that led to the tower. Its narrow windows seemed to wink at me.

When one evening after dinner I asked my mother to take me up to the tower, my parents looked at each other. It's all shut up there, my father said; it's not safe. Come here, said my mother, I'll tell you a story instead. She bent down and took me on her lap, though my feet almost touched the floor.

The only stories were family stories, and they were all the one story. As my mother told it, I could see it unfolding like a dusty tapestry, silted up with memory. How my great-grandmother had long fair hair and married a prince and had five children and lived happily ever after in this very manor house. How my great-great-aunt embroidered cloth of gold and married a duke and had four children and lived happily ever after across the mountains. How my grandmother had deep blue eyes and married an earl and had three children and lived happily ever after in this very manor house. How my great-aunt danced like a sparrow and married a baron and had two children and lived happily ever after across the seas. How my mother married my father and had me.

I liked to consider this long story and how it led all the way to me, as a path winds to a mountaintop. It soothed me for a while; it made me feel that I was in the right place, the only place to be.

But the worms of discontent had got into my veins somehow. I kept asking about the tower, no matter how they tried to fob me off. Then one evening after dinner I demanded that my father take me beyond the bramble hedge and my parents stared at each other. There's nothing out there you need to see, said my mother; it's a cruel world full of evil men. Hush, said my father, don't frighten the child. He bent down and asked, Would you like a kitten instead?

It was black and white, the softest thing I'd ever laid hands on. It was my own, more precious than all my golden toys. I cosseted it and carried it everywhere for a week before it turned and scratched me. My mother saw the mark on my wrist, and held out her hand for the kitten.

I waited all day for her to give it back. The scratch hardly hurt at all any more.

When that night at dinner I asked after my kitten, my parents looked at each other. It got lost, said my father. It wasn't a kitten any more, said my mother; it was turning into a dirty cat.

I found out from the maid that they'd given it to the manservant and told him to drown it in the well.

My parents lavished even more affection on me. My mother stroked my hair as she passed me in the corridors. Every time I came into the room, my father would open his arms and ask whether I had a smile for Papa today.

It was then that I began to fill up with rage. I was like a cloud that, though its face stays white, is slowly collecting its load of thunder and rain.

One day I was trying to make out the pictures on an old wall-hanging in the west wing when it billowed, as if possessed. I leaped back. A maid emerged from behind it, carrying an empty cup and plate. She looked startled to see me, but bobbed a curtsy and hurried away. From behind the hanging came a faraway sound that could have been laughter, or the caw of a crow. I was moving closer when I heard the dull gong calling me to dinner.

Then next day I retraced my steps; the hanging pulled back to reveal a heavy wooden door, locked fast. I put my ear to it, but heard nothing.

What I did next showed a strange cunning for a girl who had never had anything to hide. I bided my time until there came a day when my parents were walking in the garden, pointing out the best roses to each other. I took my mother's keys from where they hung, slipped away to the west wing and waited in the shadows for what felt like an hour. Eventually the maid came out, bearing what looked like a chamberpot, leaving the door unlocked behind her.

I took the stairs one by one, oddly frightened of what they might lead to. Round and round they spiralled; this had to be the tower. As I mounted I began to hear singing. The voice was faint and slightly cracked, but of an indescribable sweetness. The singer used words I didn't know, words like *hungry*, *ocean*, *grave*. I didn't know what she meant, but her song made me cry.

I forgot all my sorrow when I peeped into her room. There she sat, an old woman I had never seen before, her hands moving in and out of her song. Dirty white hair hung about her face like ivy.

Only when the last note was breathed out did she look up. She didn't speak, only watched me like a cat.

I cleared my throat. What is that thing that whirls so? I asked, for something to say.

Nothing but a spinning wheel, she answered with some amusement.

And that?

Have you never seen a distaff?

No, I told her.

How do you think thread gets spun, girl?

I don't know.

What do you suppose your dress is made of?

I have never given the matter much thought, I said stiffly.

She held out the distaff. Wrap your hands around the length of that now, she said. And she howled with laughter as if at some joke I had missed.

I walked past her, to the window. The sill was thick with dust; light sparkled in a cobweb. From here I could see far beyond the bramble hedge. There was what looked like a river, and a few lines of little houses, and in the distance, great purple things I thought must be mountains. I was so involved in identifying these things from pictures I'd seen that I didn't notice the old woman get up.

I can tell you're curious, she said, stretching her arms above her head. She waved at the stool.

Clearly she had no idea who I was. I must not do any sort of work, I told her.

Why's that then?

I am delicate, I explained with a hint of severity.

Delicate, my arse! she said. What do you mean by that?

I blinked at her. What is an arse?

This is, she said, stepping closer and giving me a light smack with her open hand.

I recoiled. My eyes bulged. I must go now, I told her.

What's there to hurt you in a bit of work? the old woman asked.

I mustn't, I told her urgently. My mother says, my father says ...

Her face was merry no longer. She put one foot on

her stool and leaned closer. Listen, girl, she said, they've tried to stop me teaching any of the things I know. Now they're trying to prevent you from learning all the things you don't. But gifts can only be delayed.

I don't know what you mean, I said hoarsely.

Look at those long spinster's fingers! she exclaimed. You're made for it. Take off those foolish gloves for a moment.

I examined my white hands through the mesh. But I might dirty them.

She made a rude sound with her lips. What do you know of dirt, little precious, swaddled up in gold since the day you were born? Oh yes, I've heard of you; the maid brings up what news there is. You have everyone in this castle walking on tiptoe for you, don't you?

After a moment I gave a small nod.

Not a baby is allowed to cry, she drove on, not an old man allowed to cough for fear you'd hear. All those with wrinkles or even a touch of a limp are kept out of your sight for fear they'd sadden you. There cannot be dust anywhere, or a washing tub, or a single spider.

I was distracted by a faraway thudding. It seemed to come from the bottom of the stairs. Were they scouring the house for me?

Wake up, princess, snapped the old woman, clapping her hands in front of my nose.

A tear began to well up in my eye, but I held it back. None of what you say was of my choosing, I told her coldly. I was a child.

And now?

Now I am almost a woman, I went on, my voice spiralling, and if I had my way –

She let the sounds trail away before saying, Yes? If you had your way?

I didn't know what to say. I sat down abruptly on her grimy stool. After a while I put my hand to the wheel; she showed me where. I set it in motion. There was a long moment of glorious whirling, and then I felt the needle drive itself into my finger. I screamed like a baby.

The old woman leaned over me, cradling me, hushing me. Her hair was soft like wool. I sucked the drop of blood from my finger. I never knew it would taste so like silver.

Her voice was shaking. I thought she might cry, and stared up at her, but then I realized that she was rocking with laughter. I shoved her away. How dare you?

That always happens the first time, she said through her merriment. Every time.

You knew, I bawled.

Not at all. No one knows the future.

I reached out and kicked her spinning wheel into the corner. Badness was running through my veins like wine. I hate you, I shouted. You sit here, in your dust, your foul mess . . . I'll have you punished. I could have your head chopped from your shoulders.

But what a mess that would make, she murmured.

I stared at her. My eyes were swollen with water. My head felt as if it were about to break open like an egg.

The old woman gave me a most peculiar smile.

I heard feet pounding the stairs, and a call that sounded like my name. I turned to the door and pulled the bolt across. All of a sudden I felt quite awake.

I bent over for the spinning wheel and set it back in its place. I sat down on the stool and said, Please. Show me how.

When I had got the knack of it, I asked,
Who were you
before you came to live in this tower?
And she said, Will I tell you my own story?
It is a tale of a voice.

XII

The Tale of the Voice

IN THE DAYS when wishing was having, I got what I wished and then I wished I hadn't.

I'll make no excuses; I was a grown woman when it happened to me. I'd already ripped out my first grey hair, and refused two neighbours' sons who thought they could have me for the asking. I'd learned every song my mother could teach me.

I was standing in the market the day I saw him. I stopped trying to sell my father's bagful of fish. I stared at the stranger for hours, across baskets of salmon and the shifting backs of cattle, but he never glanced my way. He stood at the side of his merchant father like an angel come down to earth. All the neighbours saw me watching, but what did that matter now?

His eyes were black like ink; mine blue as the sea. His hands were pale, gripping purse and quill; mine were scored red with fish-scales. His boots looked like they'd never touched the ground; my toes were caulked with mud. He was as strange to me as satin to sackcloth, feathers to lead, a heron to a herring.

Up to that day I must have been happy. Happy enough, at least, never to wonder whether I was or not. My sisters didn't use such language as we gossiped over our gutting knives and wiped wisps of brown hair out of our eyes with the backs of our hands. My mother, when she took a heavy basket from my arms, never searched my face. My father's eyes were cloudy as he flexed his fingers by the fire. Smiling was for Sundays.

The morning after I saw this man in the marketplace I woke up sick to my stomach and decided I was in love. If I didn't choose him, who was ten times better than any I'd ever set eyes on, I'd never choose. If this wasn't love, then it would never happen.

All the signs said it was. I was mulish and quarrelsome. I turned up my nose at cold porridge, and let my sisters finish the pickled cod. And the strangest thing: when I lay that evening at the green edge of the crumbling cliff below our cottage, facing into the mist, I couldn't sing a note. My throat seemed stopped up with the thought of him.

The man was everything I wasn't, hadn't, couldn't. Grace was in his smooth boots, and sunlight ran along behind him. His collar gleamed like a halo; he made me think of trumpets, and horses, and the flash of high gates. If I couldn't have him, I'd have nothing.

Which was all too likely. He was gone back to the city, and no one I knew had ever been to the city. They said bad things happened there. But nothing bad could happen to a man like that; the city would be a garden at his feet. Women would bloom at the sight of him. Even if I went there, what could I say, what could I do? What would draw his lips down to my salty skin?

So I went to the witch, as desperate girls do. Everyone knew where she lived, in a cave on the headland. I had never been there before; I had never needed anything they said she could give. The fishermen told all sorts of stories about her: that her cave was lined with the bones of drowned sailors, with skeleton legs for a door, skeleton hands for bolts, and a full mouth of teeth for a lock. They said that she fed sea snails from her own mouth, and was an octopus below the waist. One of them claimed to have seen her once, taking a bath in a little pool with her tentacles spilling over the rocks. They claimed she could turn men to limp fish with a single glance of her watery eye. Anyone who climbed as high as the mouth of her cave would freeze there on the rock until the witch hobbled down and magicked him into a gull to wheel and scream for eternity.

They said so many things about her, they couldn't all be true. Girls in trouble were not put off by stories.

Still, my breath laboured in my chest as I climbed along the headland. My hands shook a little when I stopped outside the cave. She was there before I realized it: she had been standing in the shadows. She was everything I half expected: a stoop, a stick, a wart on her nose, a whisker on her chin. Her white hair had a trace of red like old blood on sheep's wool. Her nails curled like roots. Her eyes were oysters in their shells, and her voice had the crackle of old nets.

And yet she surprised me. Is he worth it? she asked.

Worth what? The climb?

What climb? she said dismissively. I meant the price.

He's worth any price, I said, steadying my breath.

Glad to hear it.

I studied her suspiciously. How did you know about him? I asked.

There's always a him, she pointed out. A girl comes here for three reasons. To catch him, to quicken his blood, or to bring on her own.

He's not a fish, to be caught, I said angrily.

So that's it. The witch yawned, baring a few black teeth. Tell me now, what would you do for him?

I stopped to think. If he was drowning, I said slowly, I suppose I'd jump in the sea to save him. I'd forget father and mother and sisters for his sake. I'd ... I'd weave nettles with my bare hands.

Not particularly useful in this case. She sighed. No point my telling you he's not worth it, I suppose.

You've never seen him!

I don't need to, little girl. I've seen enough men in my time. Whoever he is, he's not worth what you'll pay.

But –

But I can see by your face that you're sick for him. If he was ugly as Lucifer you'd still see the sun shining out of his breeches and the stars in the leavings on his plate. No matter how greedy he may be you'll think everything belongs to him by right. No matter how stupid he is you'll think he converses like an angel. Am I right?

I have to have him, I told her coldly.

Good, good, she said, a girl who knows what she wants. Tell me now, how big a job will this be? Does the man like you, at least?

I flushed a little. I think so.

She peered closer. I've got a ring on my finger that tells me if it hears a lie.

I haven't spoken to him yet, I said in a rush.

The witch made a short bark I could only think was a laugh that was out of practice. I stared at her fingers, bare of rings.

This must be love indeed, she said, if you know nothing about him. This must be the real thing, if there's not a pinch of truth in the brew.

This is the truth, I shouted. I want to walk where he walks. To walk in his world, down there in the big city. For his eyes to catch on me when I'm dancing.

Go dance for him, then; what's stopping you?

No, I said, stamping my foot on the turf. You must change me first. Make me better. Make me right. Make me like a woman he could love.

She knotted her hands in her frayed shawl. What's wrong with you, girl, that you would make yourself over again?

Everything.

Change for your own sake, if you must, not for what you imagine another will ask of you.

I'm doing the asking now, I said.

A gull screamed; we watched it flap by.

After a moment, I asked, Is it possible, then?

She turned her palms up to the sky. Anything's possible.

It felt like a victory. I stood up straighter. I have no money today, I told her, but if you'll give me a little time –

She ignored that. It'll cost you your voice, she said.

I stared at her.

You won't be able to laugh or answer a question, to shout when something spills on you or cry out with delight at the full moon. You will neither be able to speak your love nor sing it with that famous voice of yours.

But –

But you will have him. Also, she said, while I was still taking a breath, there will be pain.

Pain?

Like a sword cutting you in half. You will bleed for this man.

Yes, I said all in a rush, before my other selves could stop me.

The witch gave me a gentle smile. Well done, my child.

Then I have chosen rightly?

Not at all. But I have a weakness for brave fools. She looked around her for a thistle, came close to me and combed my hair with it. Then she turned to go into the cave.

I stood like a stone, bedded in the earth. She looked over her shoulder. Yes?

Don't you ... don't I ... isn't there something we have to do?

What? she said wearily. Should I make you vomit up your voice and bury it under the cliff? Pull it out of your mouth like a silken rope and seal it in a jar?

I tried again. All I want to know is, when will it happen?

She reached out one filthy finger and touched me lightly on the throat. It already has, she said. Then the shadows around the cave mouth took her in.

I walked down the hill, my cold ears ringing.

At first I could hardly believe that the change had happened, but soon I had proof. My mother saw me packing my bundle, and asked what I was doing, but when I tried to answer her I found my throat was sealed tight as a drum. At last she understood and shrank back on her stool. One of my sisters turned angry, one mocked me, another wept as I set off from our cottage, heading into the mountains.

I walked and walked. Whenever I would have liked to sing I counted sheep instead. After a day I could no longer smell the sea. On the third day I immersed myself in a mountain lake, and when I stepped out I was white as the wind. I wound wild roses in my hair. Men who passed me on the road turned their heads to stare. It was all true, the witch had done what she promised. By the time I reached the city I had no more fear. I sold all I had for a new dress that reached to the ground whispering as I walked. Power was ringing through my lovely body: what need had I of words?

I found him easily, by walking down the street of merchants to the tallest house and sitting on the steps. After a while he came out with his father. As soon as he saw me he laughed. He said something to his father, and ran down to help me up. My feet were like raw meat, but my smile held his eyes. He was just as I had remembered. It was I who had changed. When he offered me his hand, I felt completely new.

He was sure he'd seen me somewhere before. I was a puzzle to him. After a few days he began to call me his little foundling; how the words were sweet to my ear. He didn't seem to mind that I answered all his questions with kisses. He gave me silk slippers for my feet, and a huge velvet cushion to sleep on when he was busy with his work. He took me to feasts and balls in castles and ships. Sophisticated women laughed behind their fans; I took it as a sign of jealousy. Clothed in his gaze, I could not be put to shame. When he was not dancing with me, his eyes rested on me dancing.

And one night in absolute darkness my flesh opened and swallowed him up. He made a sound like a dog. I burned as if I were being split in two. I was glad I had no voice to scream; I would have woken the city.

I couldn't walk for a day or two after. I felt like some strange seaweed washed up on my bloodied velvet cushion. He was so sorry; he brought me trays of sweets. At night, following his whispers in the darkness, I began to learn about pleasure. Every day I woke up a little altered.

After a while I would have liked to ask when we were going to be married. My eyes put the question, but all his did was kiss them shut. That was the first time I felt the loss of my voice.

But I was coming to realize that my predicament was not unique. At the balls he took me to there were many beautiful young women who didn't say a word. They answered every question with a shrug or a smile. If champagne got spilt down their dresses they only sighed; when the full moon slid out from behind the castle they watched it in silence. I could not understand it. Had they sold their voices too? Even their bodies were silent, always upright, never loosening their lines. They walked like letters on a page.

I had no fear, the evening my new life began to fall apart. I was dancing with all the grace I had, happiness stretched like a scarf around my shoulders. I turned to find his gaze, but for once he was not there. I walked through the ball, my smile unfaltering. Was he hiding from me for a game? Was he busy, perhaps, telling his friends about our wedding? The night was warm, scented with blossoms. On such a night love should be sung aloud.

When I found him on his back in the garden he was not singing, but whimpering in delight. I couldn't see which girl was on top of him: her smooth head was turned away.

You will laugh to hear how shocked I was. I had so trusted the witch's bargain, I never thought to wonder how long it would last. How I would like to be able to say that I turned and walked away, out of the ball and out of his life, stripping his presents from me step by step. Instead I must admit that I crouched there, watching, for the little eternity it took.

Later I went home with him, as always. He read nothing, it seemed, in my eyes; the night was dark.

Without a word from me or even a shake in my voice, how could he tell my heart was cracking apart? The velvet cushion under us was still soft. My legs around his waist must have been as warm as ever.

How should I blame him? How was he to know what mattered to me? Perhaps we get, not what we deserve, but what we demand. His sweet dumb little foundling asked so little of him, and that little was so easy for the flesh to give, why should she get anything more?

Some nights he came home, some nights not. On one of the nights he lay beside me, sleeping like a child, it occurred to me to kill him. There was a knife in his belt, hanging on the chair. It could all be over in a moment. If I drank from his throat, might it give me back my voice?

Whether it was love or some other weakness that stayed my hand I will never know. I stole away before morning.

After a week without food I began to follow the only trade open to a wordless girl. The men were not as gentle as he had been, but they could do me no further damage. I reeled from one day to the next, working for a mouthful of food at a time. What a fish out of water I was now, gulping on the cold streets as if every breath would be my last.

How could I stay here? Where else could I go? I was betwixt and between, spoiled for every life I could have lived. Always I would be restless now. Always I would know what I was missing.

I stayed through the winter, long enough to fill a jar with my tears. Their taste reminded me of the sea. I never thought I'd miss the smell of it, but finally, come spring, I did. I didn't know how to send a message; all I knew was the way home. The days of walking were like knives under my feet.

I made straight for the witch's cave, and threw stones into its clattering darkness till she came out.

I said you'd catch him, she remarked, leaning on her stick as if we were resuming an interrupted conversation. I never said you'd keep him. There's no spell long enough for that.

I threw another stone; it went wide. She didn't flinch.

Your sisters were here, pleading for you, she said.

My eyes widened.

They sold me their hair. She let out a snort. It was their idea; it seemed to make them happy. They've woven it into a shawl to keep me warm this winter.

I stared as she pulled the dark covering closer around her shoulders. They asked me to bring you home, she went on, and give you back your voice.

I tried to speak but couldn't.

She came a few steps closer. I don't have your voice, you know, she said softly. You do.

The flints were digging into the insides of my fists.

Your songs are still out there on the clifftop, hanging in the air for you when you want them. She paused, searching my face. Wish to speak and you will speak, girl. Wish to die and you can do it. Wish to live and here you are.

I don't understand, I croaked at last. My throat hurt.

She yawned. Your silence was the cost of what you sought, she said; it had nothing to do with me. What would I want with your voice? The music you make has always been in your own power.

Then why did you take my sisters' hair in exchange?

She smiled wickedly. People never value what they get for free. Having paid so dearly, your sisters will treasure you now.

I gathered up all the months of pain and spat. It landed at her feet. As I trudged down to the village, my sisters ran out to meet me. Their cropped heads soaked up my tears.

My mother had no words of greeting, only arms

thrown round me like ropes. I watched my father among the fishermen bringing the boats in. I would never again leave this harbour that smelt like home.

At the end of a week my feet had healed. By the next spring my sisters' hair had grown long again. Yet another year went by, and I married a fisherman with green eyes who liked to hear me sing, but preferred to hear me talk.

Climbing to the witch's cave one day, I called out,
Who were you
before you came to live here?
And she said, Will I tell you my own story?
It is a tale of a kiss.

XIII

The Tale of the Kiss

I KNOW WHAT they say about me: the gulls bring me all the gossip. Knowing what they say about you is the first step to power. Contrary to what you might half believe, I am no monster under my skirts. I grew up in a place much like this one, though half a year away. When I was the age that you are now I was a girl like you, though not quite as stupid.

There was another difference: my bleeding was meagre, when it came, and by the time the cough carried off my mother I no longer bled at all. This gave me reason to think about my future. As far as my people were concerned, women like me had no future. I knew what they thought of women past bearing; unless they had sons to honour them and daughters to clean them, they were old rags tossed in the corner.

A barren woman was hated even more; the way they saw it, she had never earned a bite of bread.

But I was not going to become an old rag, when every hair I had was still red as a lobster in the pot.

I could of course have lied and smiled, got myself a sturdy husband. The men had started lurking near our door as soon as my mother was taken bad. I could have sunk my nails into one, girded him to me and kept him hoping and cursing year after year, even pointed the finger at some other woman for looking crossways at me and hexing my belly. But I wouldn't stoop to that. So after they buried my mother, I packed up all the herbs in her store and came away.

I found myself a cave on a headland, above a village like this one. It's three months' hard walk from here, but they fish and spin and make up lies just like your folk. The cave had been lived in before; there was an old blanket, and a water bag, and a dip in the floor hollowed by many small fires. I had rock to my back and the sea to my face, driftwood to burn and the odd fish to fry. I had time to wonder now, to unpick the knotted ropes of my thoughts. I could taste freedom like salt on the breeze. There was no one to nurse, no one to feed, no one to listen to but my own self.

I thought no one would ever bother me again and I could live out my life like a gull, like a weed, like a drop of water.

What I found instead was power. I never sought it; it was left out for me to stumble over. Only a matter of weeks had gone by before I began to find presents left outside my cave. The first was a clutch of eggs; I thought for a moment some extraordinary chicken had flown up to bring me dinner. Next came a thick slice of meat, wrapped in a cloth to keep the birds off. The villagers left their offerings at first light, before I stirred out of my cave.

I thought such goodness had never been known in the whole world. I thought these were presents freely given to keep a stranger from starving. How was I to know that they were payments in advance?

It was a small boy who gave me the first hint. He threw seaweed into my cave until I came out with a big stick. He screamed when he saw me and ran until he fell over, then got up and ran again.

When he came back the next day, he was braver. He asked, What happened to the old one?

The old what?

Witch. Have you got her locked up in her cave or did you boil her in her pot?

This is my cave now, I told him sternly. There's no one here but me.

So it was a witch they were wanting. I laughed to myself, that first day, as the little boy ran down the headland, but soon enough I learned how to be what they needed.

It was not an arduous job. Mostly they left me alone with my herbs and my thoughts, but every few months one of the villagers would creep up the headland after sunset and call out, Are you there?

Are you there? the cave would echo back at them.

Will you help me? The voice more strangled now, the echo shaking. I've brought something for you ...

And only then, when they were sweating cold as dew, would I emerge, step by slow step, a black scarf over my head to hide the fact of my youth. Not that they ever looked at me properly: they seemed to think my eyes would scald them. They stared at the muddy ground while they poured out their stories of sickness, envy, grief and hunger. I never said a word until they were sobbing.

Sometimes what they needed was simple enough. To the sick, I gave potions that could do them no harm and might make them well if they wanted it enough. To the grieving, I gave words of comfort and a drink to make them sleep. To girls with terrible secrets, I gave herbs to make them whole again.

As for the guilty, spilling their burdens of malice and shame outside my cave, I thought at first that they were asking for forgiveness, but I soon found it made them uncomfortable. Punishment suited them better. They liked me to curse them. May weeds spring up where you walk! May a tail grow in the middle of your chin!

There was a woman who'd never said a kind word to her husband since she woke up the day after her wedding. I flayed her with my tongue until she burst into tears and ran home to make his breakfast. There was a man who'd not slept for ten years for thinking of what he had done to his own daughter. I told him to sell every animal he had to make up her dowry. Once there was a stranger who half smiled as he told me the worst thing he had done in his life, and then something worse than that, and then something even worse. I let him talk all night; I never said a word of judgement. His eyes flickered on my face as he talked, as if searching for something. The sky lightened and I was still watching him. My eyes moved nearer to the cliff edge, and just as the sun was coming up the stranger let himself fall into the pointed waves.

I was a little shaken that day. It was the first time I felt the reach of my power. Power that came not from my own thin body or my own taut mind, but was invested in me by a village. Power I had to learn how to pick up without getting burnt, how to shape it and conceal it and flaunt it and use it, and when to use it, and when to still my breath and do nothing at all. Power these scaly-fingered fishwives and their wiry husbands could have used themselves, if they'd only known how, but instead they told themselves how helpless they were, and came and laid power at my feet. As well as eggs, of course, and new-baked bread, and even gold coins if I judged that it would take a terrible price to make them believe in their cure.

And so the years passed, leaving little mark on me except the first grey fingerprints on my bright head. When the occasional petitioner came up the headland I answered their questions with my eyes closed. I preferred the days when I was alone. I could recognize the cry of each kind of bird; they never changed. All that was different about me was that every year my needs were fewer. My bones grew hard as iron. I tried out every herb I found, till nothing could surprise my stomach. I got so used to sleeping on stone that it no longer seemed hard to me. I rolled up in half a dozen blankets and wrapped my arms round my ribs like pet snakes. Nothing touched me in the night except the occasional spider. I was complete.

I should have known. You can't live on a cliff for that long without risking a fall.

One morning a woman climbed up to my cave before dawn. I could hear her feet scrabbling outside. The sun was high in the sky before I rewarded her patience by standing in the entrance. Her narrowed eyes distinguished me from the shadows, and she jerked back.

You want something, I told her, a little hoarsely; my voice was out of practice.

She looked behind her for her basket.

I don't fancy butter, I said.

It was a lucky guess. She flinched. Then what will you have?

The truth, I told her.

Her hands fought like crabs. I have a daughter, she began. A good strong red-haired daughter, but she is a trouble and a trial to me. Before sunrise she's roaming the hills. I have a terrible fear she's lovesick. She gets a strange look in her eyes. When we're working I catch her singing songs I've never heard before, and where could she have got them?

I yawned, to hurry her up.

If you saw her you'd understand, the woman went on in a rush. She's no fool, nor idle; it's only this restlessness. She could be the best of daughters, if she'd only quiet down.

And her sisters?

All gone. This one's my last, you see, said the woman, her voice subsiding. I'm not getting any younger. I need to know for sure that she'll stay with me.

I turned my face away. I will consult the oracles, I told her; that always stunned them into silence. Come back at moonrise on the third day and you will have your answer.

That evening at sunset I was sitting in front of my cave, consulting the only oracle I knew, the orange sky, when a man climbed up the headland. He seemed too tired to be afraid. He stood a little distance from me.

You want something, I said without moving my head.

Yes.

Is that a fresh trout in your hand?

It is.

Toss it over the cliff, I said, just to amuse myself.

He paused a moment before unwrapping it and

throwing it towards the setting sun. A gull caught it with an incredulous shriek.

Out with the truth now, I said.

His foot dug into the chalky grass. I have a daughter, he began. A fine tall red-haired daughter, but she is a trial and a trouble to me. Half the evening she walks along the beach by moonlight. She gathers seashells like a little child. There's a friend of mine has an eye for her, but whenever he comes courting she's behind her mother's skirts in the kitchen. I have a terrible fear she'll end up an old maid.

My eyes were wandering.

If you saw her you'd understand, he went on furiously. She's no fright, nor feared of men; it's only this restlessness. She'd make my friend a fine wife, if she'd only settle down, and then he says he'd give me half shares in his big boat.

Why not one of her sisters?

All married. This one's my last, you see, said the man, his voice beginning to crackle. I'm not getting any younger. I need to know for sure that she'll do what I say.

I stared at the soundless gulls. I will consult the oracles, I told him. Come back at moonset on the third day and you will have your answer.

The next morning I woke with my head full of scrag-ends of dreams. I doused it in sea water. Today I would need all my wits. Between the mother and the father I had to pick my way carefully. I knew what happened to meddlers who came between man and wife. I knew there were some in the village below who, after strong liquor, talked of blocking up my cave in the night.

By midday rain had covered the headland. I sat in my cave, trying to persuade my little fire to stay alight. At least bad weather kept me private, shielded me from the village below with all its wearisome tribulations.

Or so I thought, until she appeared in the mouth of my cave, between curtains of rain, the girl herself, unmistakable, her blood-red hair glued to her wet throat.

It was the first time in all those years that I let another human being step across the threshold. I even lent her a blanket to stop the shivering. To make up for this softness, I unsheathed the blade of my tongue. If you're the girl I think you are, I began, staring into the struggling fire, I hear you're nothing but trouble.

She nodded as if I had remarked on the weather, and continued combing out the red ropes of her hair with a bit of old comb I'd found her.

You're not child enough for your mother nor woman enough for your father. You don't work or play or think as they would have you work and play and think.

She smiled at me with teeth like quartz.

What are you good at?

I don't know yet, said the girl, staring into the fire. Faint steam was rising from her.

What is it you want?

Nothing, she said, half laughing.

There is no creature under the sky that does not want, I told her severely.

Only what I've got, then, she said.

That's lucky.

And time to think about what I want next.

I nodded judiciously.

And time to just think.

There's plenty of that up here, I remarked.

She stared round the cave. There must be all the time in the world here, she said wonderingly.

My heart was beginning to thud.

And time to not think, I need that too, she added.

I had one more question. What do you love?

She took a deep breath, as if her list was long, then she let it out in a sigh. Everything, she said.

Everything? My voice was a squeaking bat. How can

you love everything before you know anything, you idiotic girl?

I don't know, she said seriously. It seems to leak out of me. It's like a cup spilling over. She turned to look into my eyes; they narrowed against her. How can you not? she asked.

What?

You're wise. You're the witch. How can you look at everything and know everything without love?

My heart was pulling on my ribs. Go now, I said. The rain's eased.

She turned her open face to me. But will –

Girls like you always get what they want.

Her full-throated laugh filled the cave for several minutes after she'd gone.

That night I didn't sleep at all. The blankets were heavy with damp; the wind seemed to whine at the cave mouth. No matter which way I lay, stones poked me awake.

If I took a fever and lay tossing here till I died, I realized, no one would ever know. The villagers would still leave the odd bit of food outside, but it would be eaten clean by the birds. Only the wind would hear their petitions, and perhaps its answers would be wiser than mine.

Before the sun rose I hauled myself up off the floor. As long as I had my health the power was mine. I threw rosemary on the fire and breathed in its clarifying air. By moonrise I had concocted my answers. To the mother I said: The oracles tell me that because of your own faults, a terrible curse has been visited upon your daughter. If you ever order her to stay at home with you, she will turn into a hare and run off up the mountain.

Dumbstruck inside her shawl, the woman whispered, Is there any cure for this curse?

Only time will wear it out, I told her.

I would take no payment. I watched her scurry down the headland. I sat there as the moon tracked its way across the sky and began to fall.

To the father I said: The oracles tell me that because of your own sins, a dreadful fate has fallen upon your daughter. If you ever order her to marry, her husband will turn into a wolf and devour her on their wedding night.

Flinching from the words, the father said, Is there any way of lifting this fate?

Only time will tell, I told him.

I would take no payment. I watched him stride home. And then all was quiet. I told myself that the job was well done.

Over the next few days I went about my business, but something was wrong. Everything I cooked tasted bitter. My daily tasks seemed long, and yet when I sat by the fire to rest in the evenings, the time hung heavy on my hands. I could make no sense of what the gulls were saying.

The girl came back one day. I hadn't realized it was her I was waiting for. I almost wished it was raining again. In sunlight she glowed as if her hair had caught fire. I stood in the mouth of my cave, and all at once I couldn't think of anything to say.

She put down her basket and crossed her arms a little nervously. I wish I knew where you get your power, she remarked. This past week my mother and father have let me work, sleep and wander as I please. They make no complaint or prediction, cast neither my past nor my future in my face.

I allowed a small smile to twist my mouth.

Have you put them under a spell? she asked.

An easy one; you could learn it yourself.

She remembered her basket. I brought you something.

No need.

It's only butter. I made it myself.

I don't want butter. It gives me a rash, I said, the lie coming easily to my lips.

What'll you have then? she said. Because I owe you.

A kiss.

I think I asked it just to shame her. I would have liked to see that calm face furrow up for a moment. But the girl laughed.

Anger began to clamp my teeth shut.

Her laugh rippled on. Is that all? she asked. Why are they all so afraid of you, when your price is so easy to pay?

Even then I didn't believe she would do it. Kissing a witch is a perilous business. Everybody knows it's ten times as dangerous as letting her touch your hand, or cut your hair, or steal your shoes. What simpler way is there than a kiss to give power a way into your heart?

She stepped up to me and her hair swung around us like a veil.

It was a bad idea, that kiss I asked for. Not that it did the girl any harm. She walked off across the hills as if she had just embraced a cat or a sparrow. Once she looked behind her and waved.

On the whole I am inclined to think that a witch should not kiss. Perhaps it is the not being kissed that makes her a witch; perhaps the source of her power is the breath of loneliness around her. She who takes a kiss can also die of it, can wake into something unimaginable, having turned herself into some new species.

Days passed, somehow. There was a long red hair on my shawl that was too bright to be mine. I tried to get on with my life. I did all the same things I had done day by day for years on end, but I couldn't remember why I had ever done them, or indeed what had brought me here to live alone in a cave like a wild animal. I tried not to think about all that. I tried not to think.

I woke one night. The moon was full, filling the mouth of the cave. All at once I knew I needed that girl like meat needs salt.

What could I do? Could I bring myself to follow her down into the village? Could I lower myself so far, to let the little children throw sand at me? Would she be gone away by the time I came down? Would they tell me where she had gone? Would I be able to find her?

And if I did, I swore to myself, swore on the perfect disc of the moon, then I would not let pride stop up my mouth. I would ask her to come live in my cave and learn all I knew and teach me all I didn't. I would give her my heart in a bag and let her do with it what she pleased. I would say the word love.

And what happened next, you ask? Never you mind. There are some tales not for telling, whether because they are too long, too precious, too laughable, too painful, too easy to need telling or too hard to explain. After all, after years and travels, my secrets are all I have left to chew on in the night.

This is the story you asked for. I leave it in your mouth.